Edgar & Ellen®

MISCHIEF MANUAL

Edgar & Ellen®

MISCHIEF MANUAL

AN EXPERT'S GUIDE TO PLANNING, PERPETRATING, &
PLAUSIBLY DENYING ALL PRANKS GREAT & SMALL
(BUT MOSTLY GREAT)

Scribbled by
EDGAR & ELLEN

Edited by
CHARLES OGDEN

Cobbled together by
RICK CARTON

ALADDIN PAPERBACKS
New York   London   Toronto   Sydney

Watch out for Edgar & Ellen in:

Rare Beasts
Tourist Trap
Under Town
Pet's Revenge
High Wire
Nod's Limbs

ALADDIN PAPERBACKS
An imprint of Simon & Schuster Children's Publishing Division
1230 Avenue of the Americas, New York, NY 10020
Text and illustrations copyright © 2007 by Star Farm Productions, LLC
All rights reserved, including the right of reproduction in whole or in part in any form.
ALADDIN PAPERBACKS and related logo are registered trademarks of Simon & Schuster, Inc.

Designed by Star Farm Productions, LLC
The text of this book was set in Bembo.
Manufactured in the United States of America
First Aladdin Paperbacks edition June 2007
10 9 8 7 6 5 4 3 2 1
Library of Congress Control Number 2006036303
ISBN-13: 978-1-4169-3935-1
ISBN-10: 1-4169-3935-0

TABLE OF CONTENTS

THIS BOOK REALLY ISN'T MY FAULT. The other ones—*Rare Beasts* and *Nod's Limbs* and everything in between—those, you may attribute to me. But the blame here must lie squarely at the twins' footied feet. They've written every last word of this screed themselves on crumpled scraps of ink-blotted paper; all I've done is collect the scraps and assemble them in the most logical order.

You'll recall Edgar and Ellen, of course, from the books I've written about their mischievous misadventures. And you'll also recall the advice that precedes every story—very wise advice indeed:

IF EVER IN YOUR LIFE YOU ARE FACED WITH
A CHOICE, A DIFFICULT DECISION, A QUANDARY,

ASK YOURSELF,
"WHAT WOULD EDGAR AND ELLEN DO?"

AND DO EXACTLY THE CONTRARY.

Well, truer words were never writ. In this book, Edgar & Ellen hope to rope you into some ill-conceived scheme to prank the world one person at a time . . . or possibly all at once, I can't be quite sure. Heaven help you if you wish to join them in their folly—you won't emerge from their world unscathed.

Spoken from experience,

—Charles Ogden

TWINTRODUCTION:
THE LEAGUE OF MISCHIEVISTS COMETH!

by Edgar & Ellen

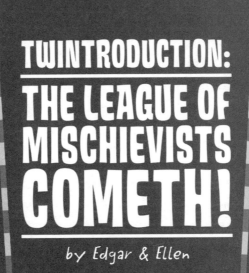

Imposters. Imposters, everywhere!

Ever since we've gained a little notoriety from our exploits (published fictions, televised stories, a fanatic-fueled Internet frenzy, and so on), we've been flooded with reports of copycats trying to steal our glory as the **Most Accomplished Mischief Makers in the World**.

Yes, copy *us*. We, the creators of the infamous *Reverse Flush* device. We, the masterminds behind *Operation: Bakery Fakery,* the worst upside-down cake catastrophe of the last decade. We, the joint winners of the coveted *Misery-Lover of the Year* award from the **Society of Schadenfreude**.

Yet somehow a plague of *Edgar & Ellen* competitors is creeping forth like an infestation of slipgibbet weed. Swindlers and attention hogs like these are giving honest deceivers and schemers a bad name:

> **BOO!** **Medgar & Melanie**, the Icelandic "performance artists" who made headlines by dumping a load of frozen codfish into a harbor. Yes, *dumping*—they didn't even use a giant slingshot! Newsflash, wannabes: Codfish *belong* in the harbor, so your prank was pointless.

No offense to slipgibbet weed; it's my favorite wildflower. —Ellen

Hector & Helen, a pair of trivial pretenders who claim credit for our successful prank, *Operation: Cut the Custard*, and are demanding we cease and desist the imitation of their "act." Act? There is no ACTING on the path to glory, friends. On the advice of our legal counsel, we say: "Go sit on a pin!"

And then, those scoundrels: The **Kats-in-Jammies Kids**. Whatever you do, DO NOT buy their frivolous book, *101 Paths to Pandemonium*, which is full of second-rate advice, tired squirting-flower gags, and worst of all, a flat-out misleading title: The "paths" they promise might lead to *disorder*, perhaps zig-zag past *disturbance*, but land nowhere near *pandemonium.*

We forewarn you to avoid their other books—dreck and doggerel, with names like Rare Beef, Tourist Tripe, Blunder Town, and the wretched Pat's Revenge, just to name a few. —E&E

See? Nothing but shams and charlatans as far as the telescope can see. Well, we have news for those people:

> *We hereby declare you fakers* **TARGET #1** *in our perpetual battle against know-it-alls, stuffed shirts, goody-goodies, and* **especially** *uncreative counterfeiters.*

How? How can we possibly hope to quash this surge of copycats spreading over the globe faster than festering throb-toe fungus? Simple: We're recruiting our own army of loyal henchmen.

That's right, Generalissimos Edgar & Ellen are calling all practicing (or potential) pranksters to join the **League of Mischievists**, a global network of havoc-wreakers under our thrall, all of whom will have been properly trained in the Mis-

My favorite fungus. —Ellen

chief Arts. Think of the possibilities! If we say *jump* in Juneau, Alaska will tremble; if we say *onward* in Oslo, all of Scandinavia will cower. Let's see any of those phony-baloneys achieve such planet-spanning influence! They cannot. They will not. They *dare not.*

And *you*—you could be a secret agent in this scheme, an essential cog in the machine of our merriment.

If you qualify. That's a big *if*. After careful charting, graphing, plotting on paper (Edgar), and some shouting and foot-stomping (Ellen), we've created this humdinger of a book that will screen you, train you, and test you on our patented approach to the Mischief Arts.

"Gasp!" you gasp. "Your trade secrets will be secret nevermore!"

Oh, don't worry about us. We still hold all the cards here, and there's no way in Nod's name we'd give up *everything*. What we share in this tome is just enough to encourage you to *think* like us, *plot* like us, *make mischief* like us. We've kept entire swaths of our true genius in reserve; you'll see that for yourself...*if* you can prove your worth. That's what this book is for.

So fie, frauds! Fie, bastions of boredom! Fie! Fear the coming of our twinly wrath! Behold, *The Edgar & Ellen Mischief Manual!*

—Edgar & Ellen

CHAPTER 1:
PRANKSTERS AT THE GATES
(BUT WILL WE LET YOU IN?)

1

So you want to waltz right into the ranks of the **League of Mischievists**, do you?

Well, cork up your beakers, pal—we don't let just anyone enter our elite corps of chaos. There's a lot of sensitive information in this book, so we've set up a bit of a screening process to keep out the—let's put it gently—*less than worthy*. If you can't get through this quiz, you can forget it.

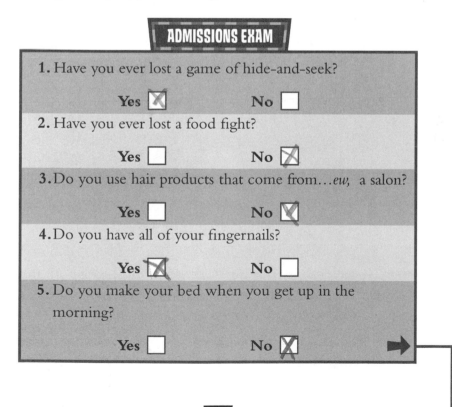

ADMISSIONS EXAM

1. Have you ever lost a game of hide-and-seek?

Yes ☒   No ☐

2. Have you ever lost a food fight?

Yes ☐   No ☒

3. Do you use hair products that come from…*ew,* a salon?

Yes ☐   No ☒

4. Do you have all of your fingernails?

Yes ☒   No ☐

5. Do you make your bed when you get up in the morning?

Yes ☐   No ☒

6. Are you afraid of spiders?

Yes ☐   No ☒

7. How about gorillas?

Yes ☐   No ☒

8. Mice?

Yes ☐   No ☒

9. Barnacles?

Yes ☐   No ☒

10. Do you adore your hometown?

Yes ☐   No ☒

11. Can you tie a Three-Fingered Violist's Knot?

Yes ☐   No ☒

12. While blindfolded?

Yes ☐   No ☒

13. Do you own a thrabo-static Grubine generator?

Yes ☐   No ☒

14. Have you ever fashioned a wax duplicate of yourself in order to escape an unpleasant duty?

Yes ☐   No ☒

15. Do your pajamas have footies?

Yes ☐   No ☒

16. Are you wearing your pajamas right now?

Yes ☒   No ☐

17. Do you have a diabolical monologue memorized?

Yes ☐   No ☒   ➡

18. Did you just shout *"Yes!"* and launch into your diabolical monologue?

Yes ☐   No ☒

19. Have you been doing it for ten minutes now?

Yes ☐   No ☒

20. What's the square root of an owl?

Yes ☐   No ☒

SCORING:

The correct answer to questions 1–10 is **NO**. The correct answer to questions 11–20 is **YES**.

20 correct: Congratulations, you scored a perfect Edgar. Now close this book and go away. There's no way you scored that well without cheating and lying to us about it. Off with you!

19–11 correct: You're in! You're unpredictable; edgy; a risk-taker. We like the cut of your jib.

10 correct: This would also mean 10 wrong…hmm, weird symmetry…something ominous about that, don't you think? OK—you're in, but we're keeping an eye on you.

9 correct: No way. You can't join. Why? Because part of being a Mischievist is being unpredictable. So, beat it, Nines!

8, 6, 4, 2 correct: You're in.

7, 5, 3, or 1 correct: You're out.

0 correct: You're not even trying. You expect us to work with raw material like this? Give it a little *oomph* next time…

In case you were wondering, I didn't take the test. I'm already a Mischievist, I get to break the rules. —Ellen

By the way, an extra point for sheer gall. —Edgar

For those of you who have been dismissed, go get your priorities straight and try again later (Hint: Settle into some well-worn footie pajamas before you retake the test). For the rest of you, we solemnly declare you **Boots in Training**, and there you will remain until you earn the right to call yourself a Mischievist.

Read on, if you've got the grit!

"WHAT'S IN IT FOR ME?" YOU ASK...

What's the point of all this pranking? Why bother getting up off the couch, slinking all over town, building complex engines of mischief, and hauling them to the roof of Town Hall in the dead of night, all at the risk of detention, or grounding, or worse?

Simple: The world needs us. It desperately needs to be made more fun, to have someone knock it on its heels, turn it upside down, shake it up, go gonzo on it. Enter the Mischievist: We exist to give dull, complacent people a collective smack upside the head. For their own good! Really.

Our brand of merry mayhem is not done out of spite—that's too easy, and anyone can be mean.

Let us repeat: We are not bad guys. Bad guys break into little old ladies' houses to steal their heirloom jewelry. Bad guys knock down your house to build highways or airports. Bad guys make giant robots to help them take over the whole planet.

If *we* broke into a little old lady's house, it would be for much-needed redecoration, like gluing all her furniture to the ceiling. If we had an airport to build, you could bet we'd leave your house there (so we could crop-dust it with sour milk). And you can be sure that if we had an army of giant robots under our thrall, we would...okay, that would be pretty cool.

It boils down to this: the world can be a boring, stuffy place. We've figured out how to keep it worth waking up to.

Have you?

CHAPTER 2:
PROFILES IN
PRANKSTERISM

(WHICH ONE ARE *YOU*?)

2

Hey, Edgar, tell them the drawbacks of getting rejected by the League of Mischievists. —Ellen

Not all Mischievists were created alike. If you think got-your-nose jokes are the pinnacle of humor, then yes…you might technically qualify as a prankster. But you're not League material. Only the best of the best make it into our camp.

If you passed our rigorous screening test in the last chapter, then you most certainly fall into one of six categories:

- **The Shifty Schemer:** The ultimate planner
- **The Impulsive Imp:** Surviving on instinct
- **The Sneakster:** One with the shadows
- **The Brute:** The force is with them
- **The Snake Oil Salesman:** Can charm your footies off
- **The Gutsy Gambler:** Lives for the thrill

You may well wonder which category that we, Edgar and Ellen, fall into. The answer is: *all* of them, chumps. As masters of our craft, we are little bits of each personality type. Equal parts raw force and subtle misdirection. In your face one moment, behind your back the next. Whoopie-cushion loud and cat's-paw silent, all at once.

You? You're lucky to be reading this book, so you'll be assigned to one of the following six cubbyholes and like it.

—They don't get to wear the cool badge. —Edgar

No, no, no—they don't get to take orders from us! That would be a tragedy. So be smart, wiseacres! —Ellen

Common Habitat: Lurking in his hideout, surrounded by mechanical odds and ends, raw chemical compounds, and numerous strange and unusual tools.

Standard Characteristics: The Skillful Schemer likes to plan every move in advance, spending long hours alone making blueprints, studying maps, and charting escape routes. Often he is interested in physical science, schematics, and complicated swindles. To the Schemer, nothing is more beautiful than a finely crafted blueprint—but because of this obsession with detail, he works best with the Impulsive Imp, who can cut through the fussiness and prod the Schemer to action.

Brain: Large and in charge.

Chin: Often rubbed, deep in thought.

Eyes: Always looking 3 steps ahead.

Hands: Smudged with ink.

Feet: Pointed toward escape.

Satchel: Houses essential equipment.

Accessories: The Skillful Schemer lives and thrives by his gadgets and gear, which he carries with him at all times, housed in a carrier the depths of which only he understands.

Catchphrase: "By jove, I've done it again!"

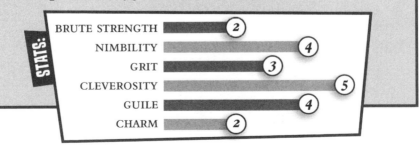

STATS:

BRUTE STRENGTH	2
NIMBILITY	4
GRIT	3
CLEVEROSITY	5
GUILE	4
CHARM	2

Common Habitat: Various. Why stay in one place too long? It dulls the creative impulses.

Standard Characteristics: Prone to rash decisions, the Imp is at home among chaos. She secretly thrills when a plan goes awry, because she excels when forced to think on her feet and use her improvisational skills. She works best alongside a Schemer, who can temper her impulses with careful thought. But once the seed of an idea is planted in the mind of the Impulsive Imp, she works quickly to bring it to full bloom before her partner has a chance to overthink it.

Mouth: Fast moving for fast talking.

Pigtail: Tug for instant reaction (wear pads).

Elbow: For nudging partner out of way during escape.

Hands: Soiled with dirt.

Missing Fingernail: Evidence of an arch-foe.

Gut: Makes most of the decisions.

Accessories: The Impulsive Imp's interests meander like a beetle, but she may always be found with an item or two relating to her new hobby (i.e., shovels, mustard, carnivorous plants, dental implements).

Catchphrase: "Let me do the talking."

STATS:

BRUTE STRENGTH	2
NIMBILITY	3
GRIT	4
CLEVEROSITY	3
GUILE	5
CHARM	3

Common Habitat: Dark corners, behind bushes, under beds, in cabinets, under covers, in plain sight

Standard Characteristics: The Sneakster is often small in stature (or extremely flexible), able to fit into teeny hiding places impractical for the rest of us. Sneaksters are often inscrutable—what do they want? Who are they working for? It's always hard to say...but they can befriend anyone they want since they are (seemingly) so agreeable. A master of camouflage, the Sneakster makes an excellent spy, pilferer, and the classic "fly on the wall."

Eye(s): Peeled.

Hair: Slicked for speed.

Nose: Sniffing out trouble.

Hands: Deft and dexterous.

Feet: Silent as church mice.

Lips: Sealed.

Accessories: Few; Sneaksters travel light to stay nimble

Catchphrase: "..." (It's amazing how memorable utter silence can be.)

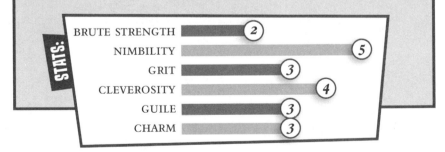

STATS:

BRUTE STRENGTH	2
NIMBILITY	5
GRIT	3
CLEVEROSITY	4
GUILE	3
CHARM	3

THE BRUTE

Common Habitat: Playgrounds, school hallways, locker rooms, and bike racks

Standard Characteristics: The Brute relies on a trove of classic (but lame) gags he uses over and over and over (famous ones include the *Tripping Foot*, the *Untimely Shove*, the *Your-Shoe's-Untied*, the *What's-That-on-Your-Shirt*, the *Hertz Doughnut*, and many, many more). He is usually big, beefy, and thick of neck—his size and strength give him free rein to play without fear of retaliation. The Brute often has one or two loyal minions, and an entire school of classmates who loathe him.

Accessories: Fists; lackeys, rolls of nickels

Catchphrase: "Why are you punching yourself?"

Backpack: full of copied homework.

Mouth: How can one sneer and snarl at the same time?

Elbow: Always jabbing partner—"Didja see that?"

Hands: Balled at all times.

Stride: Confident. Commanding. Wide.

Feet: Prone to fake karate kicks in your face.

STATS:

BRUTE STRENGTH	5
NIMBILITY	3
GRIT	4
CLEVEROSITY	3
GUILE	4
CHARM	1

Common Habitat: Front of the classroom, inside the principal's inner circle, behind the counter of the ice-cream store

Standard Characteristics: By the time you are finished talking to the Snake Oil Salesman, you will be convinced that it was your idea to fill up your house with reclaimed dog poop to start a mushroom farm. She will talk you in so many circles, you'll be standing in the center of a bull's-eye, which is exactly where she wants you. Authority figures love her; she's the most pleasant kid in class—most deceitful, too. While she is no stranger to perpetrating her own brand of pranks, the Snake Oil Salesman specializes in "buttering up" targets for her partners, then sitting back to watch the show.

Eyes: Never break contact with yours.

Voicebox: Equipped with powers of supreme sincerity.

Smile: Disarming, sweet, duplicitous.

Handshake: Firm (but make sure you still have your watch).

Clothing: Never gives the wrong (that is to say, right) impression.

Accessories: Sticks of gum (for sharing/buying influence), friendship bracelets

Catchphrase: "Well, aren't you a sight for sore eyes!"

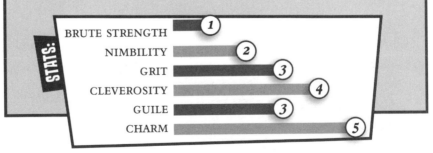

STATS:

BRUTE STRENGTH	1
NIMBILITY	2
GRIT	3
CLEVEROSITY	4
GUILE	3
CHARM	5

Common Habitat: The middle of everything, especially trouble

Standard Characteristics: The Gutsy Gambler fears nothing. He's the guy you send to the rooftop precipice to fasten the pulleys to the gargoyle; the guy who thinks nothing of running into a birthday party dressed as a piñata to create a diversion; the guy who will stuff hot dogs in his shoes to lure the pack of guard dogs away from the Point of Prank; the guy who would stow away in the trunk of a monster truck just for the opportunity to sneak into the garage after the rally. Why? Not only for the thrill, but also the pride in knowing that no other prankster has the grit.

Eyes: Steely, unblinking.

Brow: Unsullied by sweat.

Heart: Always beats at the same rate.

Chin: Thrust upward in an "I'm not scared of you" kind of way.

Spine: More than anyone.

Belly: Possibly black & blue, but never yellow.

Accessories: Parachute, bungee cord

Catchphrase: "All you had to say was *dare*; there was no need for *double-dog*."

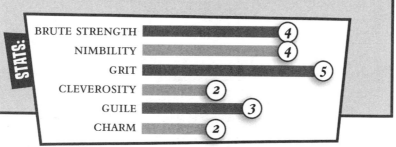

STATS:

BRUTE STRENGTH	4
NIMBILITY	4
GRIT	5
CLEVEROSITY	2
GUILE	3
CHARM	2

There are two ways to find out what role you will fulfill in the League of Mischievists:

METHOD 1: THE NEVER-MISS, MEGA-PERCEPTIVE, ONE-QUESTION APTITUDE TEST

Answer this question, and be brutally honest:

You and your partner are filling the gymnasium up to the rafters with pistachio gelatin, when Principal Dewgood catches you in the act. Which phrase are you most likely to mutter?

A. "Stand your ground...we can bull our way out of this."

B. "Quick! Shinny up the rope and we can swing out the window!"

C. "No worries. We've gotten out of worse."

D. "My patented Springheel Autoboots will bounce us to safety. Hold on!"

E. "When he gets close, switch the hose to maximum. If we're going down, he's coming with us!"

F. "I'll butter him up with the old _Have You Lost Weight_ approach. We'll be out of this in no time."

If you picked **A**... you're a **Brute**
If you picked **B**... you're a **Sneakster**
If you picked **C**... you're a **Gutsy Gambler**
If you picked **D**... you're a **Skillful Schemer**
If you picked **E**... you're an **Impulsive Imp**
If you picked **F**... you're a **Snake Oil Salesman**

METHOD 2: THE BUREAU OF ELECTRONIC PRANKSTER ASSESSMENT

Not satisfied with your results? Not convinced we've got you pegged? Never fret, we provide a second option that's the electronic equivalent of popping your brain out and slipping it under a microscope.

Our patented profiler is available on the World Wide Interweb, especially for those of you who like cyberspace, digital ether, and all that virtual reality. Visit:

www.edgarandellen.com/mischiefmanual

TEMPTING TARGETS

The most common types of quarry for practicing Mischievists:

THE INSUFFERABLE SNOOT

These snooty kids think they deserve special treatment—and you're just the one to give it to them! But beware: though they're slow to react (they can't *believe* they've just been splattered with mud!), they will soon snap into action…usually with a pretty extreme comeback. If a Snoot finds out you're responsible for a prank, be prepared to have an archenemy on your hands. Their grudges last forever, and they have the resources to support the battle.

Hey, did you know there's a spot on your shirt? These guys don't— just like they don't remember this gag from the last time you pulled it. The Dupe falls for your traps every time. When you're hitting a rough patch, and some of your best-laid plans have gone astray, give yourself a treat by duping a Dupe. "Hey, wanna do me a favor? Stand over here on this X." You'll feel better in no time.

THE ETERNALLY OBLIVIOUS

The Eternally Oblivious see the world as they'd like it to be, ignoring anything, including a particularly juicy prank, that might ruin their day. Yes, they're easy **marks**, but attempts at pranking them often yield unsatisfying results; you may have soused them in soap suds, but they'll just shrug and be glad their clothes are getting so clean. The more optimistic Mischievist might view this target as a tantalizing challenge.

> **MARK:** Your target; the lucky individual who's pegged to get splattered with bits of his own birthday cake (heh heh heh).

THE UNPRANKABLE

Oh, they make tempting targets, with all that oddball behavior and seeming unawareness of the world around them. But these guys are wise to your dodge, even before you think it. Avoid at all costs! There's not a projectile, pit trap, rope snare, or fast-talking grift that has ever gotten the best of an Unprankable. How do they possess this super-shaman sixth sense that stifles your best-laid plans? *How?*

A true Mischievist can look at an everyday item and think of at least 7½ ways to use it. —Edgar

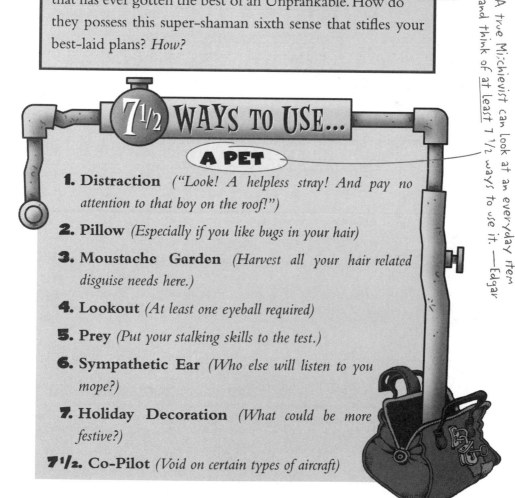

7½ WAYS TO USE...

A PET

1. Distraction *("Look! A helpless stray! And pay no attention to that boy on the roof!")*

2. Pillow *(Especially if you like bugs in your hair)*

3. Moustache Garden *(Harvest all your hair related disguise needs here.)*

4. Lookout *(At least one eyeball required)*

5. Prey *(Put your stalking skills to the test.)*

6. Sympathetic Ear *(Who else will listen to you mope?)*

7. Holiday Decoration *(What could be more festive?)*

7½. Co-Pilot *(Void on certain types of aircraft)*

CHAPTER 3:
PREPARING FOR PANDEMONIUM, INCLUDING P.P.P.P.P. AND OTHER REPEATING CONSONANTS
(ROME WASN'T DESTROYED IN A DAY)

It's one thing to talk about pranking. But before you go into the field with a wheelbarrow of muffin dough and a half-baked plan, you must do your homework. Yes, the dreaded H-word! Only the laziest of mischief-makers—or the ones with very low goals—can avoid study of our Art.

Thus we begin with the **Six Ps:**

PROPER PRIOR PREPARATION PREVENTS POOR PRANKERY

Aside from being some totally silly alliteration that Ellen just came up with, it's solid advice. And we're here to guide you through this Proper Prior Preparation before you end up Pickled by Poopy Planning. Try to keep up.

OBEY THE MISCHIEVISTS' CODE

By definition, Mischievists are an unruly lot, dedicated as we are to the High Principle of causing chaos and promoting bedlam. This is why some degree of order and agreement is necessary when perpetrating a prank. Mischievism is more than an art, it's a profession. And we have our own ways to keep things professional.

"Bedlam" comes from a nickname for the Hospital of St. Mary of Bethlehem in London, which was a lunatic asylum starting around the year 1400. Who says history is useless? —Ellen

Pranksters the world over have long sworn allegiance to a set of all-encompassing rules known as…

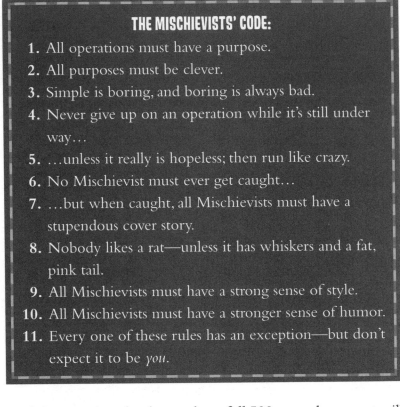

THE MISCHIEVISTS' CODE:

1. All operations must have a purpose.
2. All purposes must be clever.
3. Simple is boring, and boring is always bad.
4. Never give up on an operation while it's still under way…
5. …unless it really is hopeless; then run like crazy.
6. No Mischievist must ever get caught…
7. …but when caught, all Mischievists must have a stupendous cover story.
8. Nobody likes a rat—unless it has whiskers and a fat, pink tail.
9. All Mischievists must have a strong sense of style.
10. All Mischievists must have a stronger sense of humor.
11. Every one of these rules has an exception—but don't expect it to be *you*.

And upon full payment of your dues. Sorry, did we not mention dues? Um, don't worry about it. You'll be billed later. —Edgar

And these are just the short rules; a full 500-page document will be issued to you upon full membership in the League of Mischievists. For now, we have sprinkled this book with snippets of the complete Code to give you an idea of how serious we are about maintaining the rule of law over our minions.

Remember: Obey or pay!

Perhaps you think mischief is the kind of thing best practiced alone. "I don't need anyone's help," you say. "I don't want anyone slowing me down."

Good for you! Don't worry, there will plenty of people to socialize with in detention…*after you get caught.*

See, working alone is foolish. Partnership, at the very least, means an extra set of hands to throw the grappling hook while you cradle the smoking stinkpots—and at best, it's an extra mind to think of an escape when the stinkpots explode while you're still scaling the empty elevator shaft. Partners can distract, schlep, and even take the blame while you run off to de-stinkify (odors can incriminate, though not as well as paint or foodstuffs).

Consider these possible candidates:

• **A sibling:** Naturally. You share living quarters, routes to school, and long-distance family vacations in the back seat of the car. This gives you plenty of time to plot, scheme, and swear oaths of allegiance. Plus, if this partner betrays you—say, forgets to properly seal the cap on that jar of Zanzibar Biting Beetles he handed you—*you know where he lives.*

• **An underling:** Nefarious schemers with grandiose plans have one thing in common: they can always find some poor schmo willing to work for peanuts just for the chance to be in the presence of greatness. Underlings are the rock-star groupies of the mischief world, toiling at all hours and hauling heavy prank components and expecting only recognition in return. (Of course, all the greatest nefarious schemers give recognition like *"Faster,* you diminutive dunderhead!" or "I said the *red*

Or whatever particular torture your family prefers. —E&E

I said I was sorry! —Edgar

button, you undersized oaf!" Underlings love it, though.) You may find an underling by placing a classified ad in *Misbehavior Monthly.*

• **A pet:** Pets can act as lookouts, decoys, distractions, bait, and counterweights. (Depending on the complexity of your scheme, they could do all five.)

POTENTIAL PARTNER PETS

DOGS
Advantage: Loyal.
Disadvantage: Shedding could gum up sensitive prank apparati.

CATS
Advantage: Equipped with deadly claws and "ice in the veins."
Disadvantage: Couldn't care less about your grand plans.

FISH
Advantage: Can be trained to infiltrate underwater lairs or retrieve lost equipment from ocean floor...
Disadvantage: ...but that requires a *lot* of fish.

WEASELS
Advantage: The sneakiest mammal in the animal kingdom.
Disadvantage: Basically just a hairy snake with legs. Kind of creepy, if you think about it.

PET
Advantage: Cunning, sly, conniving, always up to something; can formulate plans independently.
Disadvantage: Cunning, sly, conniving, always up to something; can formulate plans independently.

Well, Miles Knightleigh really seems to go for that. Your mileage may vary. —Ellen

Yeah, you never really know what you're going to get where Pet is concerned. —Ellen

• **A friend:** Ha! Just kidding. Mischievists don't have friends. We only have victims and professional colleagues.

STOCK YOUR POCKETS

The greatest tool a Mischievist has is her mind—but while it's enough to survive, it's not enough to thrive (even for Ellen). You also need a steady supply of gadgets, gizmos, replacement parts, and other helpful hardware to perpetrate mayhem or escape a scrape.

> **POINT OF PRANK (POP):** The intersection of your plans with the poor sucker who doesn't see it coming; in other words, *where it all goes down* (may be indicated by big red "X" on your blueprint; painting a giant "X" at your *actual* POP is optional...but has that afore-mentioned panache).

But they must be *portable* to the **point of prank.** It does you no good to have your prototype anti-gravity generator sitting on a worktable in your lair while you're dangling from the gutters of your victim's surprisingly slippery roof!

Here's a checklist for assembling your own ready-for-anything emergency tool kit.

- ☐ **Something to carry it all in**: Backpack, briefcase, purse, carry-on luggage, library tote, carpetbag, or pocket-laden cargo pants

- ☐ **Rope** (lots and lots)

- ☐ **Oil can** (full of motor, olive, or castor oil; or a mix thereof)

- ☐ **Assorted cogs and gears** (can double as spare tires)

- ☐ **Banana peels** (in various stages of decay)

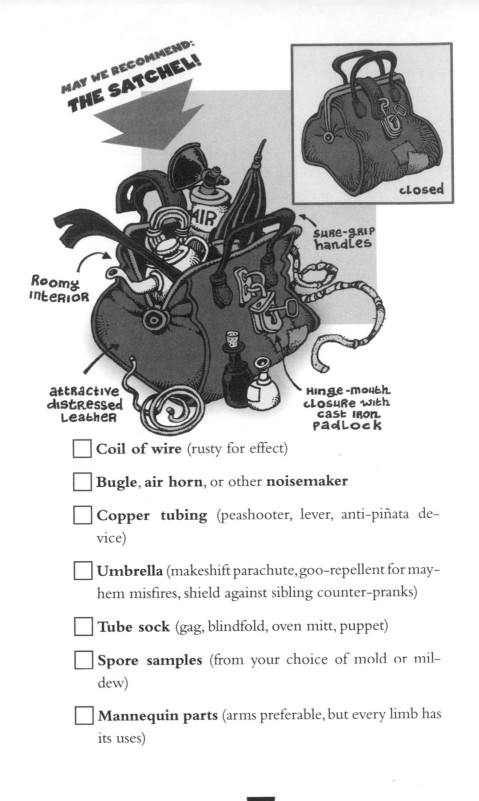

MAY WE RECOMMEND:
THE SATCHEL!

closed

sure-grip handles

Roomy INTERIOR

attractive distressed Leather

Hinge-mouth closure with cast iron padlock

☐ **Coil of wire** (rusty for effect)

☐ **Bugle**, **air horn**, or other **noisemaker**

☐ **Copper tubing** (peashooter, lever, anti-piñata device)

☐ **Umbrella** (makeshift parachute, goo-repellent for mayhem misfires, shield against sibling counter-pranks)

☐ **Tube sock** (gag, blindfold, oven mitt, puppet)

☐ **Spore samples** (from your choice of mold or mildew)

☐ **Mannequin parts** (arms preferable, but every limb has its uses)

Only 19 left in existence! Get yours while you can. —Edgar

☐ **Bandages** (first aid, emergency rope, mummy disguise)

☐ **Shark repellent** (trust us)

☐ **Gasket cutter** (preferably a 1912 Faversham)

☐ **Hat pin**, **paperclip**, or **thumbtack** (Store carefully!)

☐ **Extra-strength glue** (Store even more carefully!)

☐ **The Ladies' Auxiliary**. This is the collection of essential schemer's tools, so named because all the best tools have lady nicknames. The core tools are:

  ☐ **Bess** (crowbar)

  ☐ **Kate** (lock pick)

  ☐ **Gert** (grappling hook)

  ☐ **Jane** (headlamp)

  ☐ **Stephanie** (wad of chewing gum on some string)

BE YOURSELF...EXCEPT WHEN YOU'RE IN DISGUISE

The best Mischievists are also **Masters of Disguise**. Every prankster should have quick access to the following:

☐ **Wigs** in every style and color (Edgar looks smashing as a ringlet-tressed redhead.)

☐ **Fake glasses** (Do *not* choose models with noses and mustaches attached—those are so last year!)

☐ **Shiny badge** (doesn't matter what it says—flash it quickly and assume authority)

Just like its namesake, the stephanie quickly loses its flavors, and tends to make a mess of everything if you aren't careful. —E&E

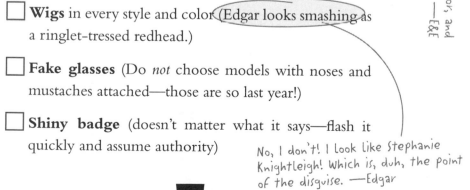

No, I don't! I look like Stephanie Knightleigh! Which is, duh, the point of the disguise. —Edgar

— Well, then, it's perfect. —Ellen

What if you're at the astronaut rodeo? —Edgar

Just be smart about it, okay? A cowboy alien with a broken leg draws too much attention to itself. —Ellen

☐ **Cowboy hat** and **bandana** (Our research indicates cowboys say "yeehaw" a lot; you may want to bring a horse as well.)

☐ **Clown suit/floppy shoes/big red nose** (useful for infiltrating birthday parties, circuses, and rodeos)

☐ **Top hat** and **cane** (good for impersonating railroad tycoons and land barons)

☐ **Wedding dress** (Act insane; everyone fears an anxious bride.)

☐ **Stethoscope/lab coat/tongue depressor** (People tend to obey doctors without question; use tongue depressor to silence dubious victims.)

☐ **"Vote for..." button** and **clipboard** (Pollsters get *all kinds* of valuable information from people—just by asking!)

☐ **Martian antennae** and **green paint** (Trust us—some people are *really* gullible.)

Don't be afraid to mix and match!

DRAW UP YOUR PLAN

Ellen has agreed to stand back from the typewriter for a while, since I, Edgar, am the primary draftsman and blueprint specialist in our household.

Drawing an official plan for your official **operation** is an absolute, no-miss requirement at all times in

OPERATION: A general term for your plan as a whole. All proper operations have a catchy, memorable code name, such as *Operation: Booger 'n' Spice*, or *Operation: Happy Barfday*.

your pre-prank preparations. Do not skip this step, even for the most basic of schemes. Don't rush it either; sloppy planning yields sloppy results. For example, here is one of the very first blueprints I ever made:

You'll notice the blueprint failed to take into account the croquet mallet that Ellen was holding in her other hand at the time. This was the crucial element missing from my planning that resulted in a thoroughly botched scheme…as well as a bright red welt.

Don't make the same mistake. Sketch out your idea to the very limits of its possibilities. If you're going to be a Mischievist, you must think of everything! With a little practice, your perfectly plotted plan will hatch forth from a blueprint that might look a little something like this:

And slooooow planning yields a bunch of stupid, unworkable blueprints that completely miss brilliant opportunities. —Ellen

Away with you, I say! —Edgar

WHAT TO DO IF YOU CATCH SOMEONE WITHOUT PROPER BLUEPRINTS

Refer to the Mischievists' Code, Section 48a–352cc: *"If, upon the execution of a plan, whether successful or unsuccessful, a Mischievist is found to have perpetrated a prank sans appropriate and properly drafted blueprints, s/he shall be obliged to subject her/his forehead to subsequent scribbles by fellow Mischievists with semipermanent and extremely smelly markers, by means of which s/he shall have drafted upon him/her the plans/blueprints for a wholly new prank. Pursuant to this, a hand mirror shall be issued to the offender, and a 24-hour window granted to execute said prank."*

POST FAUX BILLS

PHONEY SIGNS FOR CONFUSION-SOWING FUN

CRISP, NEW
DOLLAR BILLS—
50¢ EACH

7½ WAYS TO USE...

A GARDEN HOSE

1. **Belt** *(For the rather rotund)*

2. **Lasso** *(Drive them antelopes!)*

3. **Sea Monster** *(It doesn't take much to fool some people.)*

4. **Giant Noodle** *(Impress your friends!)*

5. **Insult** *(Get over here, you Garbage-Brained Garden Hose!)*

6. **Fake Snake** *(When there are no real snakes)*

7. **Mega-Snorkel Tube** *(Useful for lying low when things get hot)*

7½. **Hydro-Pressurized Anti-Prank Suppressor** *(Point and spray to keep the meddlers away.)*

CHAPTER 4:
ON YOUR FOOTIES SCUM! IT'S BOOT CAMP!
(DROP AND GIVE US FIFTY!)

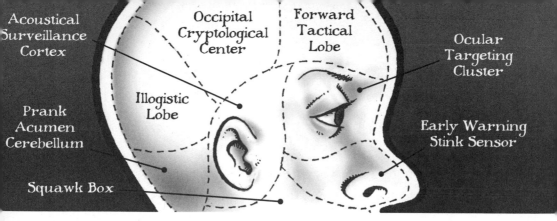

Acoustical Surveillance Cortex

Occipital Cryptological Center

Forward Tactical Lobe

Ocular Targeting Cluster

Illogistic Lobe

Prank Acumen Cerebellum

Early Warning Stink Sensor

Squawk Box

Newbies, believe us when we say there are no gimmes. Pranking like the pros comes from grueling repetition, unrelenting practice, and a drill sergeant who'll make you cry.

Consider this your Boot Camp, boots.

DRILL #1: GROW EYES IN THE BACK OF YOUR THICK HEAD

Executing a successful prank requires a heightened sense of **situational awareness**. That means pay attention! You must keep your focus on your marks while tracking their movements, simultaneously noting any changes in the weather, the quality of light, the direction of the wind, and the whereabouts of any **mushrooms** or other interlopers

> **SITUATIONAL AWARENESS (SA):** A degree of understanding of your environment at all times (attention to approaching footsteps, knowledge of neighbor's dog's whereabouts, anticipation of mailman's arrival, etc.).

who could dish up the whole works. The last thing you want is to be getting ready to launch Phase Alpha when a security guard sneaks up behind you and asks you what you think you are doing hiding in the bushes with binoculars and a miniature robot of Stephanie Knightleigh.

> **MUSHROOM:** A person who always seems to pop up at the wrong moment, threatening to endanger your plans.

Do these simple exercises to strengthen the situational aware-ness centers of your brain:

What do you mean you don't own a pipe organ? —Edgar

- Keep track of the rats that scurry by while you're playing the (pipe organ). In the parts of the song where both your feet aren't occupied with the pedals, try to pinch their tails with your toes and flip them up into the maws of the stuffed moose heads on your wall.

- Tape one eyelid shut and throw a newspaper up in the air. As you watch the pages fall, recite all of the head-lines backward before they hit the ground. Lean your head way down as it falls, if you have to, but be careful not to smack your face against the ground, because that really hurts and you look ridiculous.

- Walk into your classroom with an elephant snout fas-tened to your face and go directly to your desk. Take out a piece of paper and write down a detailed list of how all the kids reacted: who laughed, who stared, who made a dumb comment. Write down what they were wearing, how many times they blinked before you reached your desk, and what it looks like they ate for breakfast that morning. When you can't think of anything else, crumple up the piece of paper and eat it.

DRILL #2: KNOW YOUR PLAN LIKE YOU KNOW YOUR OWN SNEER

You've gone to the trouble of devising your most ingenious trap, complete with bait, decoys, fire ants, winches, and pulleys, and the ever-essential chalkboard blueprints. Wouldn't it be a shame if you got to your **red zone** with all that stuff and then forgot which jar of snakes goes on what catapult, or how many cranks to turn when?

> **RED ZONE:** The wide area around the **POP** containing the greatest dangers to your operation due to high pedestrian traffic, little or no cover, exposure to prying eyes, etc. The jig could be up from any number of directions. That means watch it!

Disaster! Make sure you study, study, study those blueprints! You will thank yourself—nay, you'll thank *us* for it later.

But there's more to truly *knowing* the plan than memorizing blueprints. You must go the extra step: You must see *through* the plan. (Cue eerie ghost music.)

Example: You are about to activate *Operation: Balloonacy* when a truckload full of nanny goats overturns in

> **AREA OF EFFECT (AOE):** The area destined to be splattered, deluged, or otherwise drenched by the impending prank.

the **AOE** of your POP. Now you have no view of the big, pink Happyloaf Cotton Candy stand you were about to soak out of existence. There is no way your Mechanical Water-Balloon Baboon can make it into range, and the plan is a bust.

Or is it? What do *you* do?

> *Edgar says: Be Patient*
> Just because a complication presents itself doesn't mean you have to abort, push the panic button, or run an inferior prank. Keep your head. It's possible the nanny goats will sniff out a tempting patch of clover somewhere and skitter out of your way in time.
>
> *Ellen says: You're Crazy, Edgar*
> There's no way this situation resolves itself, Brother. In this ➡

event, you *think of alternatives as fast as possible.* I suggest setting the water balloon contraption on Maximum Fling, and clearing the area of goaty nuisances immediately.

Edgar says: *You Fool!*
Sister, once the cotton candy people see the sloshing mayhem outside, they'll shut their shutters and lock them tight. You've given away the prank! This is an unforgivable **fudge**. Before you barrel in and spoil everything, let's think. If I remember correctly, the Nod's Limb's Gastroliscious Goatfood factory is near the Happyloaf stand. If you disguised yourself as a factory worker with a simple pair of overalls, you could sneak inside and get back with a double armload of irresistible goat treats inside of five minutes. Bingo—we've got a tasty treat to lure those bothersome billies away.

> **FUDGE:** The corruption of plans as a result of impatience. *Very irresponsible.*

Ellen says: *Ooh, Ooh, I Have a Better Idea!*
That slingshot probably has a range of about a cornfield-and-a-half if you tweak its arm length just right. You could hurl all those treats into the swirling vat of cotton candy. Now you have the perfect vantage point to sit back and watch that herd of hungry nanny goats overrun the cotton candy stand. That's even better than the original plan!

Edgar says: *I Humbly Submit*
That's poetry.

See? If you had been busy playing with your irregular beet collection instead of diligently studying your blueprints, that big truck of nanny goats would have been your undoing. Worse, the failure wouldn't have been their fault; it would be strictly **operator error**. But if you learn to think the Edgar & Ellen way, each potential obstacle becomes a majestic pathway to creative genius!

> **OPERATOR ERROR :** The determination that everything would have gone smoothly if *someone* hadn't **fudged** the whole shebang.

DRILL #3: LEARN HOW TO MOVE

On more than one occasion, we have found it necessary to hastily exit a scene through such unlikely portals as loose floorboards, heating ducts, shower drains, and mail slots. Having a wide range of personal maneuvers could save your neck—or more importantly, your prank!

So practice these classic moves:

SLITHERING LIKE A SNAKE

Advantages:
- Low to the ground: reduced visibility!
- Eliminates telltale footsteps…and foot*prints*.

Drawbacks:
- Hurts on paved surfaces.
- May draw unwanted attention from zookeepers.

Mail slots? Ellen, this never happened. —Edgar

Yes it did! You must have been elsewhere at the time. —Ellen

SLINKING LIKE A CAT

Advantages:
- Allows you to approach the target low and out of sight.
- Allows you to move silently.

Drawbacks:
- May feel compelled to nap frequently.
- If you get chased up a tree, you'll need the fire department to get you down.

JUMPING TO THE CEILING AND HANGING BY YOUR TOES

Advantages:
- A quick escape!
- A better chance of surprising your target from on high.

Drawbacks:
- Only works if you've worn holes in your footie pajamas.
- Plaster is very difficult to get out from under toenails, and if you leave it there, eventually your nails…uh, never mind.

We caused the outage to begin with, enabling us to unleash all manner of plans under cover of darkness. It was a prank-within-a-prank, really. —Edgar

FLATTENING YOURSELF AGAINST THE WALL

Advantages:
- Allows you to sneak down alleys and hallways.
- You get textured grooves in your skin if you stay still long enough.

Drawbacks:
- Doesn't hold up to closer scrutiny, especially by masons.
- May be difficult to peel self from wall afterward.

HIDING IN PLAIN SIGHT

Advantages:
- Requires no preparation.
- Relies on imperceptiveness of others, which is abundant.

Drawbacks:
- Requires no preparation.
- Doesn't work.

I mean, preparation really is the best part, isn't it? —Edgar

Yeah, don't even bother with this one. —Ellen

DRILL #4: NAVIGATE IN PITCH DARKNESS

You can cause a lot of trouble in the dark. Whereas your opponent is relying on his eyes, you, the practicing Mischievist, need to be able to enact mass mayhem without the benefit of 60-watt illumination. We pulled quite a successful prank during the Monumentally Catastrophic Power Outage of last spring. You don't need to know all the details to that one, but let's just say it took a few days for the townsfolk of Nod's Limbs to sort out whose britches were whose, and even then we don't think everyone was ever absolutely positive.

The easiest way to practice this is of course to tie a long, smelly sweat sock over your eyes and walk around the (ground floor) of the house. Try tying your shoes, making a sandwich, or writing a letter to the mayor requesting the construction of more junkyards.

Who needs eyes, anyway? Your other senses will tell you all you need to know.

Smell: Train your nose to identify people by their scents. Ellen, for example, has the pleasant odor of pickled nettle soup, while Stephanie Knightleigh stinks of lavender and jasmine and other foul musks. Helpful info to have in a darkened room.

Sound: Like a bat, you can judge your location by the sounds around you:

IF...	THEN...
Your voice falls flat in front of you...	...you're in a box.
You sploosh when you walk...	...you're in a sewer, or possibly a bathtub.
You hear deep breathing...	...you're in a yoga class.
You hear snoring...	...your partner has fallen asleep.
You hear a badger singing love songs...	...*you* have fallen asleep and now you're dreaming.
You hear mooing and the revving of jet engines...	Where exactly are you?

Taste: Lick walls and other surfaces to glean valuable information about your surroundings. Powdered-sugar residue, for example, indicates the recent presence of a baker (Have you stumbled into a pie factory, perhaps?), while a discarded action figure may bear the salty hallmark of Miles Knightleigh's sweaty little mitts (You've infiltrated the Knightleigh Manor play room! Proceed with caution!).

Touch: This is the strongest sense you have. It will let you know when water is leaking through your shoes, when you've entered a hallway lined with hidden blowdart holes, or when you've fallen flat on your face. Use these clues wisely.

DRILL #5: BUILD YOUR FIRST CATAPULT

You're ready for an important step on your road to joining the League of Mischievists: the construction of your very first medieval projectile-hurling machine. Like a sparkplug gapper to a mechanic or a melon-baller to a gourmet chef, the catapult is one of the trusted tools you'll be using time and time again in your career as a master Mischievist. Oh, the things you'll fling!

Construction is easy and relatively straightforward. Follow the diagram; using tools from your satchel and scavenged parts from your local junkyard, your catapult will come out looking just like this!

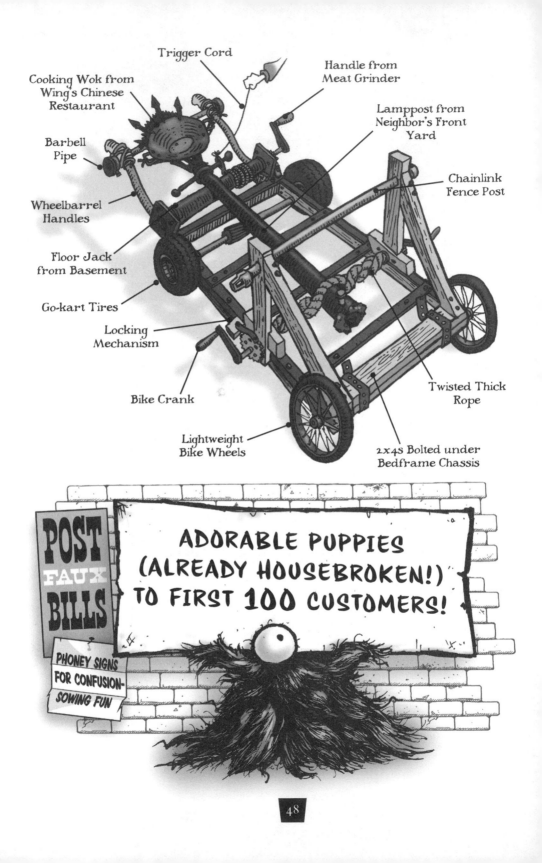

Trigger Cord

Handle from
Meat Grinder

Cooking Wok from
Wing's Chinese
Restaurant

Lamppost from
Neighbor's Front
Yard

Barbell
Pipe

Chainlink
Fence Post

Wheelbarrel
Handles

Floor Jack
from Basement

Go-kart Tires

Locking
Mechanism

Twisted Thick
Rope

Bike Crank

Lightweight
Bike Wheels

2x4s Bolted under
Bedframe Chassis

POST FAUX BILLS

ADORABLE PUPPIES
(ALREADY HOUSEBROKEN!)
TO FIRST 100 CUSTOMERS!

PHONEY SIGNS
FOR CONFUSION-
SOWING FUN

7½ WAYS TO USE...

A POTATO

1. **Missile** *(Splats nicely when well cooked)*

2. **Little Man** *(Requires nimble carving)*

3. **Sewer Plug** *(Fill culvert openings for optimum flooding.)*

4. **Shoe Filler** *(Everyone loves surprises.)*

5. **Pillow Stuffer** *(Perfect for your annoying siblings)*

6. **Phony Softball** *(Little League will never know what hit 'em.)*

7. **Secret Storage** *(Hollow it out, stow teeny valuables inside.)*

7½. **Disappearing Ink** *(Very complex chemical formula)*

CHAPTER 5:
FAST TALK FOR FAST THINKERS
(WHAT WE TALK ABOUT WHEN WE TALK ABOUT TALK)

ᴇLLEN ɪꜱ PRETTY GOOD at using words to disentangle us from a tight spot. She once double-talked a construction foreman who caught us lurking too close to the crane operator's booth. By the time she was through, the poor **bumpkin** thought we were surprise quality control inspectors from the

> **BUMPKIN:** Clod; see glossary at back of book for full definition.

Head Office, and he practically gave us the keys to the crane, the bulldozer, and the fleet of dump trucks. That would have been too fantastic for words.

Knowing what to say and how to say it can deflect trouble as efficiently as a suit of armor, so fill up your novice brain with these Mischievist quips, clips, and double-spoke-speeches.

PRATTLE LIKE A PRANKSTER

So maybe you have a satchel stocked with blueprints, hand tools, and assorted wigs. You may *look* like a Mischievist...but if you don't sound like one, you'll be laughed out of the League. We have included a glossary at the back of this book to help you make sense of the most important phrases and secret words. Memorize it in your spare time!

It's full of such helpful jargon as "foniwerd" and "maidyalook." —Ellen

Ellen has informed me (through a considerable clamp on my right ear) that the words "pretty good at" should be replaced with "an undisputed master at." Well played, sis. —Edgar

But for now, here are a few essential phrases that will have you sounding like an old pro in no time:

Useful if, for example, Ellen helpfully offers you the last cookie in the jar. —Edgar

"Cheese it!"—*Beware! We should hide this incriminating evidence and act innocent!* (Alternatively: *Run like the dickens!*)

"Down with his apple cart!"—*Knock that fellow down!* (Also useful as a verb: *"He's blocking the exit. Apple-cart him into the mud!"*)

"What's your dodge?"—*Hmm, I suspect you are trying to deceive me.*

"We've been made!"—*Alas, the authorities have discovered our scheming intentions!*

"Nunya."—*That is, I'm afraid, none of your business.* (As in: *"Where do you think you're going, mister?" "Nunya. I'll call you when I get there."*)

"I'M WITH THE MAYOR'S OFFICE OF OFFICIAL OFFICIATION, MA'AM" AND OTHER USEFUL COVER STORIES

Sometimes you get caught—hey, it happens to the worst of us. And when your **Plan B** just isn't working out, you'll need a last-ditch way to extract yourself from trouble. You need a good cover story.

PLAN B: A backup plan that comes into play in the event that a good prank goes bad. Acceptable Plan Bs include hiding, running, engaging your jet pack, and pretending to be innocent. "Praying for a miracle" is *not* considered a practical Plan B, C, D, or even E, for that matter.

When devising your own cover story, remember to develop three tiers for each; the higher the tier, the more complicated the cover:

• If, after your initial line, the interloper gives you a grimace, squint, scowl, raised eyebrow, or pursed lip, bounce your story up to **Tier II**.

• If she still has a skeptical look, move to **Tier III**.

• If **Nosy Nancy** is still unsure and about to call for backup, move swiftly to **Tier IV**, otherwise known as: run. That's right, beat feet. You're done for.

Here are some cover stories we've used with great success:

Tier I: *"Oh, this little guy? No cause for worry—I'm a zoo-keeper."*

Tier II: *"Well, of course I take my lion everywhere with me. If I left him home alone, he'd eat all of the steaks."*

Tier III: *"'Scuse me, please—the Bi-Annual Big Cat Biathalon is this weekend, and I'm late for registration."*

Tier I: *"I'm the County Covered-Bridge Inspector. Yep, this one is definitely covered."*

Tier II: *"This bridge isn't built to hold all of these smashed watermelon rinds—you'd better evacuate everyone right away."*

Tier III: *"How did all these watermelons get here? Why, that's exactly the kind of thing I'd expect the guilty party to say."*

Tier I: *"I'm taking these home with me to get them appraised."*

Tier II: *"Most people have no idea how valuable their fine lawn ornaments really are. Finding those hidden gems is what makes being a lawn ornament appraiser really worth it."*

Tier III: *"Truly, I'm quite famous in certain circles of lawn-connoisseurdom. Have you seen my show on public television?"*

Our all-time most successful all-purpose cover story:

Tier I: *"I am the viper."*

Tier II: *"I vish to vash and vipe your vindows."*

Tier III: *"Valk avay, vait avile. I vill vork vonders."*

CONFUSEYISM

Things are going smoothly on your latest scheme. The steam-powered piston has fired on cue and hundreds of frozen fish have launched into the tennis tournament just as your target makes her first serve. All you need to do now is release the sea lions to ensure complete havoc—and that's when a guy with a walkie-talkie and an attitude clamps his hand on your shoulder and asks the dreaded question: *"What do you kids think you're doing?"*

None of the cover stories you've memorized will work in a situation like this. Only your ability to fast-talk this mushroom is going to make the difference between a night in the slammer and the most memorable prank in the world. Think fast—what do you say?

This the heart of Confuseyism: improvisation skills, quick thinking, and a bunch of Confusors at the ready. "Confusors" are the words you'll need to flummox your opponent; they're used out of context, so they wouldn't *normally* be used in a situation like this, but then, Mischievists don't strive for *normal*, do we? Successful Confusors slow down your target's brain, forcing him to waste time figuring out what you just said rather than wondering why you are, say, standing in the power plant control room with a pair of jumper cables and a homemade anti-gravity laser.

So, you're about to release the sea lions…and our target wants to know what you think you're doing. What *do* you say?

"Releasing sea lions. What does it look like?" Bold! Decisive!…and not Confusey at all. You may feel brave, but it's a thin line between bravery and jail time. Besides: Think of the Mischievists' Code. You can't abandon your prank yet. It needs you! *Rating: **F** for Foolish.*

"What? Where am I? What year is it?" Amnesia? Authority figures never fall for this. You can do better. *Rating: **D** for Dim.*

"Ah! Just the guy I was looking for. Did you know someone left this crate of sea lions lying here?" Not bad. You've disarmed this intruder by appearing grateful to see him. He's confused…but he hasn't made up his mind if you're telling the truth. This is good fast talk, but *not* great Confusey. *Rating: **B** for Better.*

"Where have you been? We've got a Code Black, and you're lollygagging behind the bleachers? Get to the rendezvous point pronto, or you'll pay for this back at Central." Beautiful! You have taken command with such confidence, this sap doesn't know which way is up. Is he in trouble? What's a Code Black? Where the heck is the rendezvous point? His brain is baffled and on the defensive, and he'll do as you say. *Rating: **A** for Awe-inspiring.*

Well, the ones with amnesia do, but they're pretty rare. —Edgar

So remember, the key to Confuseyism is this: lots of weird words in a row can slow down your opponent's brain. Multiple syllables work well, as in, "You better clear out, this is an *omega acid metabolosis zone,*" or, "Are you aware of the *Fibonacci sequence protocols* in this area?" These ideas are a start—but good Mischievists rely on their own brains, so try to come up with your own words, okay?

CONFUSOR STARTER KIT

Don't worry, I'm a *Socratic methodologist.*

Are you picking up any *zero-point singularities?*

Oh no, they've upgraded this to *Situation Barnum.*

I'm checking for a *dual-pass architecture fault.*

Uh-oh, looks like we've got an *iambic pentameter breach.*

Quick, go get me the *well-tempered clavier!*

Looks like *deKooning abstractions* have gummed up the works.

SIGHTING A MOOSE

Does some authority figure have you cornered? Is he accusing you of replacing the windshield wiper fluid with mustard when, in fact, you have? This person has established a position of command over you now, and is not likely to be fooled by Confusey anymore. But Sighting a Moose allows you to hijack this conversation away from its topic to serve your purposes.

Follow the steps closely:

1. The Admission: "You know, now that you mention it, I *did* misplace my mustard. It might have ended up in the car…"

2. The Sighting: "…Wait, did you see that moose go by?"

3. The Hijack: "Speaking of moose, I saw something really interesting at the museum the other day…"

This technique comes in many other variations, such as Hearing a Cannon, Smelling a Fungus, and Sensing a Disturbance. Choose one that fits your particular style.

COLD READING: MESSING WITH MINDS FOR FUN AND PROFIT

You know those TV psychics who help people communicate with their eight-greats-grandmother, or their dear, departed pet goldfish? Chances are they've got no psychic powers and they don't talk to ghosts. So how do they do it?

They're cold readers. Cold reading is a kind of fast-talk that combines perception, wit, and misdirection. You've *got* to give this a try.

> **Technique One:** *Make some vague statements.* Let's say your mark is an oafish mayor who wants to communicate with his pet puppy that has passed on to the great beyond. You're going to get him to verify your guesses…and he'll think you're peering into the great beyond.
>
> *You:* "*I see fur…dark fur.*"
> *Mayor:* "*Yes! Noodles was white, with brown spots!*"

I know, I know…I want to believe, too. I mean TALKING WITH GHOSTS, how fantastic would that be? But yeah: These guys are bogus. —Edgar

Technique Two: *Let the mark talk as much as he wants and fill in the gaps.* What did we learn in that single statement? He had a dog named Noodles with brown spots. Repeat stuff, make some more guesses, and let your mark do the rest.

You: *"Yes, Noodles is happy. Noodles is barking very happily."*
Mayor: *"That's strange…she was always such a quiet dog!"*

Oooh—a slight mistake. But is it catastrophic? No way. For one thing, look what else we've learned: Noodles was a girl. Nice work, Technique Two! Now **Technique Three:** *Tell him what he wants to hear.*

You: *"But where she is now, Noodles barks all the time. That's how happy she is!"*

Huzzah! That's a hard one to argue with, and besides— what's this chump going to do, visit the afterlife to check if you're wrong?

Technique Four: *Throw out all the guesses you want,* and he'll wait for the one that makes sense. Follow his lead, and he'll forget your wrong guesses.

You: *"I hear a squeaking, like a favorite toy, like a bone, a plastic bone or a real bone…I see a newspaper, a slipper—"*
Mayor: *"She liked to chew on my slippers— it made me so mad!"*
You: *"Yes, she used to chew on your slippers, she ruined them, and she knows now how unhappy it made you. I see the word 'outside'—does that mean anything to you?"*

Now this is a bit of a gamble. We're guessing that there was some sort of punishment involved after Noodles chewed up her owner's slippers. But more importantly—**Technique Five** alert!—we've *repeated information provided by the mark* as if we had plucked it out of the air.

Mayor: "*Outside? Yes, she loved going outside…she had a tree she liked to nap under.*"

• Okay, a slightly different outcome than we were going for. But see what we learned? **Technique Six!** *Go with what you're given!*

You: "*Yes, I see a tree, I see a tall, shady tree that Noodles loves to sleep under now. She's very happy, barking and napping and running for as long as she pleases!*"

That no doubt leaves Mr. Mayor feeling good about his departed pooch…but more importantly, he is convinced you're the real thing.

We like to call this "sleight of mind," and the best part of all is, anyone with an ounce of wit (this could indeed mean you) can do it.

The fake swami gag can get you OUT of trouble, too. Unless you're at a Swami Convention, of course. —Ellen

Every proper Mischievist needs a hideaway, a lair, someplace to spread out blueprints, untangle twine, wind up springs, and prepare for **zero hour** of the next prank. In darker moments, a well-placed hideout can also provide a safe place to retreat in the event a scheme goes sour. Not that our schemes go sour, but yours might.

> **ZERO HOUR:** The moment of truth; time to get things rollin'. It's considered good form to have a most excellent "go" phrase to initiate the zero hour. Helpful examples include: *"Showtime!"*, *"Let's do this thing!"*, *"Look out below!"*, and *"Cry havoc!"* (Use of exclamation point is required.)

"Edgar, Ellen, do share with me your bountiful wisdom: What is the perfect headquarters?" you beseech. Well, we throw it right back at you, and ask: "What do you want from your HQ?"

"What do you mean?" you reply, slightly annoyed. "I want the best. You're the experts, *you* tell *me!*"

"Wow," we say, shaking our heads sadly. "You're edgy. You're arguing with the narrators of a book. You need to calm down."

While you go soak your head in a bucket of cold water, we'll explain the obvious. Some lairs are designed to inspire your greatest schemes; others are designed to hide your dark experiments from a world not yet ready to witness them (sad, but true!). Maybe you want room to spread out plans, or a high ceiling for assembling booster rockets, or access to a waterfall for a hydroponic radish farm…a radish farm of, uh, doom or something. The important thing is that you should choose a lair depending on your needs.

When you reach our level of Pranksterdom, you don't have to choose just one. All *professional* Mischievists keep several different hideouts for different needs…but for now, you should start small and select one from this list.

YOUR HOME

Perhaps for reasons of economy you expect to do your mischief planning in your house. Not always the best choice, but it *can* work…if you have the right kind of house.

Here are some of the drawbacks to setting up a lair in your home:

• **Bedrooms aren't very sinister.** Sure, you may have painted it black and hung up creepy posters, but your bedroom is still where you keep your underwear and comfy pillows. Not a good inspiration for nefarious plots, and not very menacing to henchmen. Henchmen aren't swayed by your need to wear clean underwear.

• **The rest of your house is vulnerable to interlopers.** Kitchen table: too public. Behind the couch: too cramped. The garage: too dim. Locked in the bathroom: someone's always knocking. The only good place for an in-home lair is the basement (see below), but if you set up next to the washing machine, expect to be interrupted a lot and asked to fold clothes.

• **Where will you store your catapult?** Think about it. Once you assemble your first medieval siege device, where will you put it? It needs to be concealed from prying eyes, yet easily accessible when it's time to bombard the ice-cream social with pinecones. Besides, a catapult is only the first of many outsized accessories you'll need to stash away from prying eyes: giant robots, sewer-adapted hovercraft, dinosaur-cloning tanks—all of the good stuff takes up room.

Let's face it, a home-based home base just isn't very impressive. To put it simply: your local Mischievists will laugh at you. We picture you in your bedroom, bunched up under your covers with a flashlight. Very unprofessional.

Yeah, yeah...we know we live in OUR headquarters. Keep reading, rookies. —Ellen

BASEMENT

It's *possible* the basement of your current house could make a suitable lair. This is the equivalent of starting a major computer software business in your garage: it makes a great story if it works, but if not, you just look pathetic. Still, there are advantages: Most basements have the perfect musty aroma other Mischievists spend years trying to perfect in their own lairs; they're murky and damp, excellent for improving your mood; and they're often lit by bare bulbs, casting the whole place in a shadowy, suitable gloom. Yay! Before you move in, however, be sure to make the following modifications:

1. Private exit. Your front door can never access your hideout! You'll need a way to easily roll the vats of smelly chemicals in and out.

2. Quick-access from bedroom. You'll need to enter your basement lair at a moment's notice. Sliding through the ductwork is an obvious choice, but that can get noisy. A fireman's pole is a good choice—just hide it behind a sliding door in the back of your closet. Install two poles if you have a sidekick—extra points if you slide into your prankster's outfit on the way down.

3. Revolving hideaway worktables. When your perimeter alarm alerts you to an incoming intruder/parent/sibling, you'll need to be able to hide stuff quickly. With a touch of a button, revolving tables spin and disappear into the walls, replaced by bookshelves and inoffensive rock band posters. "What are you doing in here?" asks the intruder. "Enjoying the latest popular albums and/or young person's fiction books," you'll say, handily throwing off suspicion.

We recommend pajamas...if you're not already wearing them. —E&E

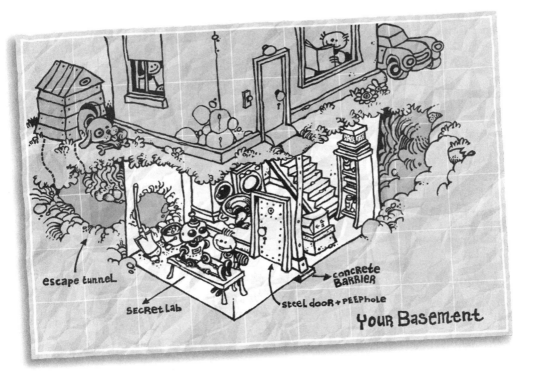

escape tunnel

SECRET LAB

concrete BARRIER

steel door + PEEPhole

Your Basement

Warning: Many houses come with parental units who like to putter in the basement. Perhaps Mother has a workbench where she builds French armoires, or Father a craft table where he glue-guns Thanksgiving centerpieces. Under no circumstances should you use your basement as a lair in this case. The interruptions would be constant, and your revolving worktables would be on permanent spin.

MANSION

Yes, we know this is technically a home, but a mansion is so far removed from that ordinary, everyday hut you live in that it deserves a separate category. So save your angry letters. A mansion, like ours, is a sprawling playground, a multi-storied terrarium

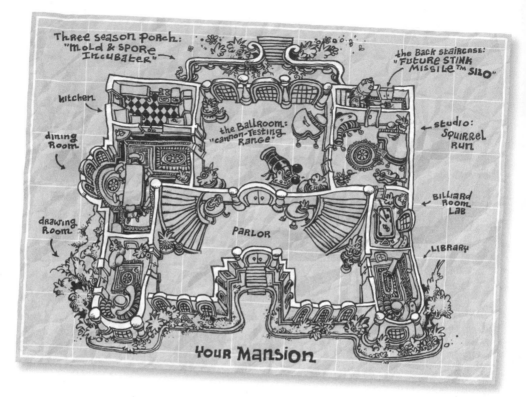

Three season Porch:
"Mold & Spore
Incubater" →

the Back staircase:
"FUTURE STINK
MISSILE™ Silo"

kitchen

dining Room

the Ballroom:
"cannon-Testing Range"

← studio:
Squirrel Run

← Billiard Room Lab

drawing Room

PARLOR

← LIBRARY

Your Mansion

for planting the seeds of genius. They come tall, affording an excellent perch from which to spy upon an entire town of potential targets, and they come wide, with interconnecting wings, effective for adding menace to your home base (as in: "I tire of our conversation. For the rest of the evening I shall retire to the South Wing—where all are forbidden entrance! Do not test me!") Some mansions have built-in security in the form of an iron-spiked fence or fancy motion detectors. Ours doesn't, but we more than make up for that with a carefully achieved look of decay and disrepair that instills dread in any would-be intruders. Plus, we like the way it looks.

Edgar, you are so weird. —Ellen

Thank you, Sister. You too. —Edgar

SEWER

Now we're talking. Sewers are the ideal hideout because they **a)** run everywhere in town, **b)** provide multiple points of exit and entry, **c)** offer total concealment when transporting suspicious equipment, **d)** come with an ample supply of rats, and **e)** are full of smells that deter lesser snoops and sneaks. To reign supreme in the underworld (doesn't that sound delicious?), you'll need your own private access, of course, so start burrowing out of your basement with a spoon—the pipes from your toilet will lead the way.

The "underground lurker" motif is a spectacular theme; here is a handy shopping list to help you get the most of it:

☐ **Gondola** *(Water travel may be your only option; gondolas are swift, silent, and thoroughly awesome-looking.)*

☐ **Torches** *(approx two to three thousand. Affix to walls every five feet throughout sewer system. Nothing inspires more awe and/or fear than a torch-lit tunnel leading the way to the heart of your lair.)*

☐ **Headlamp** *(in case the torches go out)*

☐ **Pipe organ** *(Q: What beats the sound of a thunderous pipe organ in the echoing chambers of the sewers? A: Nothing, pal.)*

☐ **Snorkel mask** *(in case the gondola tips; also useful for drain-pipe entry into your target's toilet or bathtub)*

☐ **Clothespin** *(versatile tool for plugging nose or hanging up soaked pajamas to dry)*

TREE HOUSE

Ah, the Mischievist's home-away-from-home, ever since trees and humans made one another's acquaintance. Not as classy as a mansion filled with booby traps and trick staircases, but what a tree house lacks in class it makes up for in rustic practicality. Obviously, the greatest benefit comes from the height. It's a perfect perch to keep an eye on your pranking grounds, and it adds distance to your projectiles. The tree house offers protection from snoops and prevents entry from all but the most simian invader. (But oh, those monkey intruders…beware!)

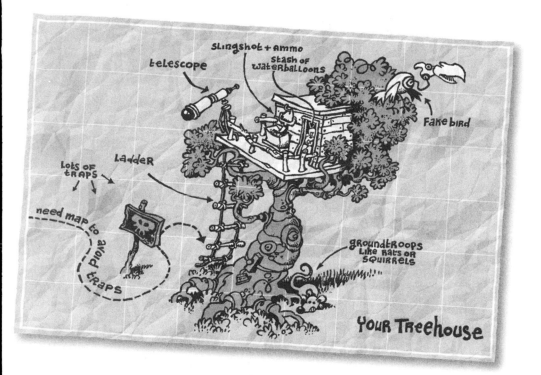

telescope

slingshot + ammo
stash of waterballoons

Fake bird

lots of traps

ladder

need map to avoid traps

groundtroops like rats or squirrels

Your Treehouse

WHAT TO DO IF MONKEYS DECIDE TO INVADE YOUR TREE HOUSE

Step One: Release your rope ladder while they're scrambling up. Some of the little boogers will go tumbling into the others below. With any luck, you could get a real simian avalanche going.

Step Two: Convince them you are a monkey, too. The only real difference is that monkeys are slightly hairier. Hunch yourself over and do the *OO OO OO* thing. If you must, pick bugs out of their hair and eat them. This should earn you some trust, which will come in handy for…

Step Three: Become a bad roommate. After they rifle through your stuff and make a complete monkey mess of your place, they'll pick some sunny spots and nap. This is when you do your best to be annoying. Hoot really loudly with your friends in the late hours, borrow their banana peelers without asking, leave the sink full of dishes. Do this repeatedly, for as long as it takes. Eventually they'll get sick of you and leave.

REMOTE ISLAND

Actually, we twins differ slightly on the usefulness of a remote island:

EDGAR SAYS...	ELLEN SAYS...
Islands give you the maximum amount of space to construct laboratories, command centers, and customized compounds.	*How are you getting to this island?*
Islands have vast natural resources such as bananas, lava and whatnot, which can be exploited to further your empire.	*Seriously, how are you getting there? You don't have a boat.*
Islands are often outside the boundaries of international law.	*And even if you did have a boat, do you know how long it would take to sail to the middle of the ocean? A long time.*
Islands usually have distinctive mountains that come in the shape of skulls or freaky tiki faces.	*And once you got there, you'd still have to come back to enact the schemes you planned. Otherwise, who would you pull them on? Monkeys?*
Monkeys! Islands are home to legions of monkeys just waiting for the right genius to turn them into loyal minions.	*Edgar, this idea is stupid.*
Also, most island drinks are served in coconut shells with a tasty wedge of pineapple.	*...*

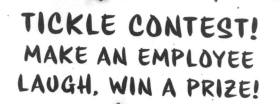

TICKLE CONTEST!
MAKE AN EMPLOYEE
LAUGH, WIN A PRIZE!

WHAT TO DO IF ANOTHER MISCHIEVIST CHOOSES TO OPERATE ON THE SAME DIGS

Refer to the Mischievists' Code, Section 6.02×10^{23}: "*Any Mischievist found to be within the pranking territory of a fellow Mischievist during the course of a respectably mischievous and/or devious operation, whether by accident or malicious and/or delicious intent, should consult immediately the condition of each other's footie pajamas, and the wearer of those pajamas with the fewer holes in the footies shall immediately submit and relinquish the territory to the "holier" of the two. Should the Mischievist be robed with clothing other than footie pajamas, that person shall immediately consign his- or herself in disgrace to the service of the Mischievist properly robed. Should neither party be robed in footie pajamas, shame befall you both.*"

We don't think we need to remind you that atmosphere is key to any self-respecting hideout. A good rule of thumb: If you would be embarrassed to host a Mischievist Convention in your lair, take a step back, rub your chin, and try again.

SURE-FIRE SIGNS YOUR LAIR IS UP TO SNUFF

- It has a mechanical stairway.

- There exist a number of trapdoors greater than the occupants are currently aware.

- Eyeballs may be removed from mounted trophy heads in order to peer into rooms from behind the walls.

- Fear of imminent doom is sustained continuously by a lunatic groundskeeper.

OUR HOME SWEET HOME

Finally, when in doubt, look to the masters. Turn the page to be blown away with the most staggering achievement in pranking architecture…

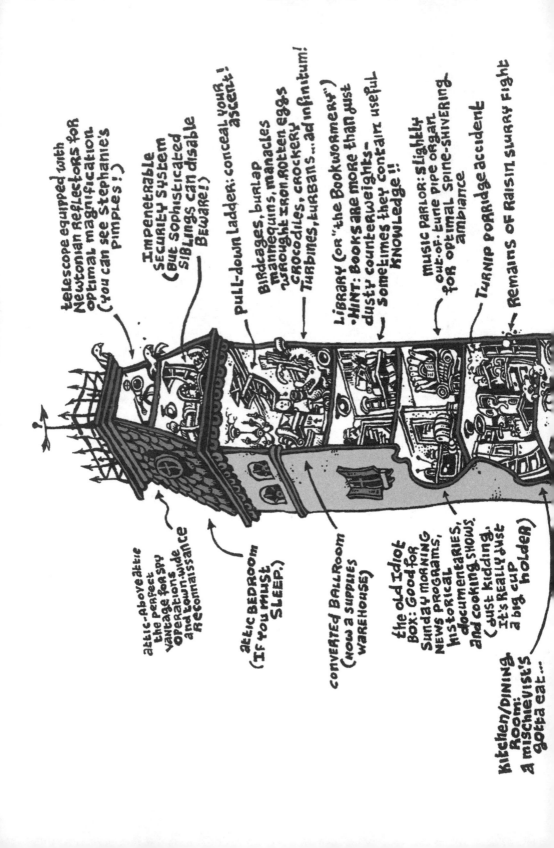

telescope equipped with Newtonian Reflectors for optimal magnification (you can see Stephanie's pimples!)

Impenetrable Security System (But sophisticated siblings can disable Beware!)

Pull-down ladder; conceal your ascent!

Birdcages, burlap mannequins, manacles, wrought iron, rotten eggs, crocodiles, crockery, turbines, turbans...ad infinitum!

Library (or "the Bookworms") •Hint: Books are more than just dusty counterweights— sometimes they contain useful knowledge!!

Music parlor: Slightly out-of-tune pipe organ for optimal spine-shivering ambiance

Turnip porridge accident

Remains of raisin slurry fight

Attic-Above attic the perfect vantage for spy operations and town-wide reconnaissance

Attic bedroom (If you MUST sleep.)

Converted Ballroom (Now a supplies warehouse)

the old Idiot Box: Good for Sunday morning news programs, historical documentaries, and cooking shows (Just kidding, it's really just a big cup holder)

Kitchen/Dining Room: Good for a mischievist's gotta eat...

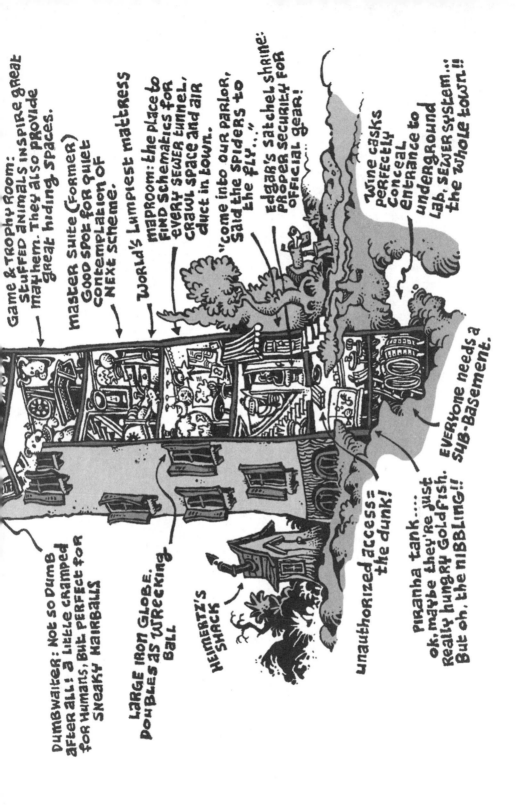

GAME & TROPHY ROOM: STUFFED ANIMALS INSPIRE GREAT MAYHEM. THEY ALSO PROVIDE GREAT HIDING SPACES.

MASTER SUITE (FORMER) GOOD SPOT FOR QUIET CONTEMPLATION OF NEXT SCHEME.

WORLD'S LUMPIEST MATTRESS

MAPROOM: *the place to FIND SCHEMATICS FOR EVERY SEWER TUNNEL, CRAWL SPACE and AIR duct in town.*

"come into our parlor, said the spiders to the FLY..."

EDGAR'S SATCHEL SHRINE: PROPER SECURITY FOR OFFICIAL GEAR!

WINE CASKS PERFECTLY CONCEAL ENTRANCE TO UNDERGROUND LAB, SEWER SYSTEM... the whole town!!

EVERYONE NEEDS A SUB-BASEMENT.

DUMBWAITER: NOT SO DUMB AFTER ALL! A LITTLE CRAMPED FOR HUMANS, BUT PERFECT FOR SNEAKY HAIRBALLS

LARGE IRON GLOBE. DOUBLES AS WRECKING BALL

HEIMERTZ'S SHACK

UNAUTHORIZED ACCESS = THE DUNK!

PIRANHA TANK.... OK, MAYBE THEY'RE JUST REALLY HUNGRY GOLDFISH. BUT OH, THE NIBBLING!!

WHAT FOLLOWS IS NOTHING MORE than a glimpse into our superior intellects, the barest peek at the fullness of our prowess. These schemes, gags, and sure-fire agitators are just enough to get you started. After you execute them properly, you'll be ready to cause your own brand of pandemonium.

But first, start small.

APPETIZERS FOR ANARCHY

So you've read a fancy-pants manual about mischief, and you think you're ready to paint the town, twin-style.

But you're as wrong as a mime on karaoke night. You need to build some confidence first with these simple monkeyshines and little gags that will confuse, confound, and otherwise tweak the people around you.

STRING 'EM ALONG

Requires ball of twine or yarn

Classic mindbender. Your mark is a sidewalk pedestrian in a city/shopping district setting. (This gag does not work well in a neighborhood or any environment where you can be seen for long distances from the Point of Prank.) ➡

1. Approach your mark and say, "'Scuse me, I'm with the City Survey Department. Mind giving me a hand? I'm trying to finish this survey, but my partner's responding to a niner-oh-seven call from dispatch. All I need you to do is hold this here string."

2. Hand your mark one end of the string. Provide these instructions: "It's very important that you stand in this exact spot"—it might be helpful here to make them move a foot or two, just to make it look more official—"and hang on tight to the string while I make a final walk-through." Be prepared to execute more convincing fast talk if your target protests.

3. Walk away while letting out the string. Turn a corner and get out of sight as fast as you possibly can.

4. When you reach the end of the string, find another mark, and repeat Steps One and Two. Then go home, laughing all the way.

This is standard Confuseyism (see page 54). Use your own best judgment for what kind of Confusor your mark will respond to. —E&E

BOOK WHO'S LAUGHING NOW

(Requires blank book, journal, or diary)

Your Point of Prank is a crowded library, study hall, or any cluster of apple-polishers who like homework and that sort of thing.

LINE OF SIGHT (LOS): An unobstructed view between two points. An **LOS** to the exploding pepper shaker: good thing. An **LOS** between Chef François and your hiding spot: bad, bad, bad.

1. Take a comfy seat within earshot of your marks (preferably within their **line of sight** as ➡

well). Open your blank book, and pretend like you're reading.

2. Laugh like crazy. Not all at once—spread it out, and let it build over time. For example, after a minute or so, chuckle. A minute later, bleat a hearty "Ha!" Twenty seconds after this, give a sustained chortle and slap your knee. Within five minutes, you should be wiping away tears and gasping for breath. Make sure people are giving you uncomfortable glances. If not, laugh harder.

3. Stand at last, and toss the book onto a table. Say to no one in particular, "They don't write 'em like that any more." Walk away. Those bookworms will never be able to resist cracking open your book so *they* can be in the know, too.

for extra credit, coat the pages with itching powder beforehand. Ha! —E&E

TOUR DE FARCE

1. With a sidekick in tow, choose an art exhibit at the museum of your choice. The more ridiculously abstract the art, the better. (Art snobs are the snootiest snobs, and are thus most deserving of our pomposity-puncturing efforts.)

2. Stand several feet back from a particularly pointless piece—say, a big round glob of red on a field of slightly different red—and gape like a love-struck dolt.

3. Wait for a fellow art lover to stroll into earshot. Then let your enthusiasm and boundless art history knowledge ➤

It's amazing what passes for art these days. What about classics like Still Life with Moldy Cabbage? Now *that's* art. —Ellen

be overheard. This is your chance to really exercise some "storytelling skills." For example: "This is Mastizmo's most famous piece from his Blue Period, when he fashioned his own brushes using fly wings and his own eyelashes. You know, all of his most important works were painted in pitch darkness—he couldn't stand the sight of his own creations."

4. Your sidekick should play the part of a rival know-it-all. Begin an argument: "You fool! Everybody knows he painted only at noon because lunch was his greatest inspiration! That's why this one is called *Egg Salad Sunshine.*"

5. Choose new painting; repeat.

WORK THE CLERK

1. Select a store where you are likely to come in contact with some smock-wearing wage jockey—don't target the boss yet. (If a manager approaches you first, abort mission.) For purposes of this example, we'll say our mark is a hardware store.

2. Ask the clerk for a thermolatrix. The clerk will not know what this is, and rightly so, since there is no such thing. "How can you not have a thermolatrix?" you say. "You must have one—it would be with the lerd-straighteners." Once again the clerk will be unable to help you.

3. Continue as necessary until the clerk reaches a low boil. "Well, if you can't find the wa-wa turbigent either, I'll have to ask for your manager," you say. "This is ➡

getting ridiculous." The clerk, used to following orders, will run off at once.

4. The manager will arrive shortly cooing phrases such as "How can I help you?" or "What seems to be the trouble?" (The clerk will be following along behind, wringing his hands.) You say simply: "I'm looking for a box of nails." If you've done your job right, the manager will spin on the clerk and holler, "What do I pay you for?" If you get any other reaction, you only get half credit, and you must select a new store and start again.

WHAT TO DO IF YOU BOTCH THE WHOLE ENCHILADA

Refer to the Mischievists' Code, Section 256 Alpha Prime: *"In the event that a prime pranking opportunity is fudged either by a) operator error or b) circumstances beyond the control of either the principal prankster or the partner prankster, then one (1) and only one (1) of the following events must follow forthwith: A) Said failed Mischievists must enact Plan B with all reasonable speed; B) an agreed-upon cover story must be employed by either member, thereby diffusing the interest of authorities, OR allowing impending escape of at least one (if not both) pranking parties (with appropriate use of costume if necessary); or C) a retreat must be made at top speed, i.e., RUN!*

If you have mastered the mayhem we prescribed for you, bravo. Bravo indeed. It's not that we were betting against you or anything.

But if these were piano lessons, the previous section was *Chopsticks*, and this next section is the *Bach Toccata and Fugue in D Minor* (with extensive use of foot pedals). In other words, there's no comparison.

Go home now. Or if you're at home already, then close your eyes, because we're worried you're not ready for...

OPERATION: SOCK IT TO METEOR
Target: your science classroom
(Requires paint, brushes, ladder, various debris and detritus, rock, and big broom)

1. In the pre-dawn hours, secure entrance to your place of education.

2. Paint a fake hole in the ceiling, with the sky visible beyond. Note: Pay attention to weather reports to mimic accurate climate patterns for the day. A blue paint job on a gray day will give it away.

3. Scatter splintered wood, chunks of plaster, and lengths of wire on the floor. Your goal is to replicate the crash site of a wayward meteor that has seemingly come through the roof during the night. Complete the look with a giant painted rock (in your choice of color scheme; fuchsia is hot in suborbital circles these days) plunked into the middle of the destruction. Hide.

4. The science teacher will open the door, take one look, and absolutely flip; some screaming could possibly occur. She will respond in one of two ways:

4a. If this teacher is a true scientist, she will jump at the chance to inspect a meteor up close. If you think this response is likely, further the confusion by bedecking the meteor ahead of time with little sculptures of "alien dwellings" and itty bitty footprints, and possibly a teeny tiny map of your town with a red X on your teacher's house. Guaranteed brain warp.

4b. If your teacher is more concerned with grading yesterday's tests rather than actual groundbreaking scientific discovery (in other words, if your teacher is normal), she will now turn and run for help. Now clean the room. Work quickly. In all you have about two minutes to sweep thoroughly and repaint the ceiling before authorities return.

5. Enjoy the rest of science class as your teacher twitches and mumbles to herself (giving you more time to plan your next scheme).

OPERATION: GOGH THE DISTANCE
Target: art museum (Works well in conjunction with Tour de Farce prank, above)
Requires raw ground meat ➡

1. Starting with your meat of choice, fashion a lifelike ear. You can do it. Michelangelo had to carve whole bodies from marble, so how hard can it be to mold an ear out of some beef? (Expert Tip: Ground hamburger can be separated and reattached with ease, though Italian sausage excels at holding its shape.)

2. Artfully display this ear in a picture frame, shadow box, or on a simple sheet of construction paper. Make it pretty—it's got to look like Art.

3. Stealthily enter your local art museum, and affix your masterpiece to a wall in any gallery. Place this sign beneath it:

VAN GOGH'S EAR

MEDIUM: HUMAN FLESH ON CANVAS
RECOVERED FROM GROUNDS OF THE
VAN GOGH ESTATE, CIRCA 18—

---

4. For a variation, cook the ear lightly (and gently). After planting it in the museum, wait for a crowd to form… won't take long! While the mob gawks in silent, morbid awe, elbow your way to the front and, after a moment of feigned curiosity, grab a hunk off the ear and taste it. "Surprisingly salty!" you'll say over the shrieks.

OPERATION: THE PARROT AND THE STICK
Target: any parrot owner

1. Every evening after your mark has gone to bed, quietly remove the parrot from the premises.

Yes, Vincent van Gogh cut off his ear to show some lady how much he loved her; it's the grossest (and therefore most famous) story in all of art history—even grosser and more famous than the tale of Picasso and the bean burrito. —E&E

2. Back in your lair, train the beast (using the standard principals of Behavioral Modification and Reinforcement Theory; don't tell us you don't know them) to mimic the sound of a doorbell. Return parrot before dawn.

3. Repeat the following night, and so on for three to seven months.

4. Eventually, the target parrot will make such a convincing doorbell sound—and will be conditioned to make it so frequently—that your mark will go bonkers answering the door every five or six minutes. (Yes, the effort is worth it. If you had to ask, you shouldn't be holding this book.)

WIN $10 IF WE FORGET TO OFFER YOU A FREE BACK-SCRATCHER!

POST FAUX BILLS

PHONEY SIGNS FOR CONFUSION-SOWING FUN

CHAPTER 8:
FLUNK OR FLY?
A FINAL EXAM
(SEE HOW YOU MEASURE UP)

Don't mark up the library's copy, you fool! Librarians are Unprankables. They'll track you down! They have skills! —Ellen

Lo! If you've made it this far, you might just have what it takes to join our ranks. Unless you're one of those rotten book flippers who skips around and reads whatever you want—you need to go start over at the beginning, pal, because it's test time! What, did you think this was all in good fun? Mischievism isn't some hobby, you know—it's a way of life. So grab a ballpoint pen (don't worry about marking up your book; you can always buy another copy, rate yourself on these questions, and see how you stack up as a Master of the Mischief Arts.

1. The best way to start a food fight is to choose a target, toss some food, and let them assume it came from somebody else. They'll return the favor and the food fight will have begun. But which fruit or vegetable do you start with?

☐ **A. Potato**

☐ **B. Tomato**

☐ **C. Squash**

☐ **D. Bundt Cake**

Answer: B. Tomato. It's squishy and red, and will splatter on contact. A potato is hard to aim, the squash'll probably slip out of your hands, and the bundt cake will more than likely make your target happy.

2. You've decided to pants the school bully and show the world his boxers. He's unsuspecting, and you have ample opportunity. But where do you do it?

☐ **A. His birthday party**

☐ **B. His *mother's* birthday party**

☐ **C. At the bus stop**

☐ **D. Gym class**

Answer: D. Gym class. The perpetual problem with pantsing is this: belts. But in gym glass you're guaranteed a quarry wearing one thing: elastic waistbands.

3. You've cracked open a few dozen cans of dog food and you're ready to swap them out with the sloppy joes in the school cafeteria. When do you make the swap?

☐ **A. Early morning, before the lunch ladies arrive**

☐ **B. Late at night, after everyone has gone home**

☐ **C. Just before the lunch bell rings**

☐ **D. *During* lunch**

Answer: C. Just before lunch. The lunch ladies will all be outside comparing tattoos, too distracted to notice you switching out their hard-sloppied joes.

4. We prank because:

☐ **A. We must.**

☐ **B. They deserve it.**

☐ **C. Life is more interesting that way.**

☐ **D. All of the above**

Answer: C. Life is more interesting that way. If you didn't get this one—come on, did you even read the book?

5. You've escaped from class and have to get to the school nurse's office to coat all the bandages with sneezing powder. All of the hall monitors have been issued a photo of you and have been put on full alert. How do you avoid them?

☐ **A. Stack up a bunch of chairs and climb to the ceiling, shinnying along the rafters until you're right above the door to the nurse's office. Wait until the hall monitor walks by, drop down, then go in and complain of a borwoolie ache. Find the bandages stash while the nurse looks up "borwoolie" in her medical books.**

☐ **B. Use air ducts to reach principal's office. Grab the intercom microphone, then announce to the entire school that Moon People have landed in the playground and are demanding to know why they're not in the school's science books. Make your way to the nurse's office once everyone has left school to see the invasion.**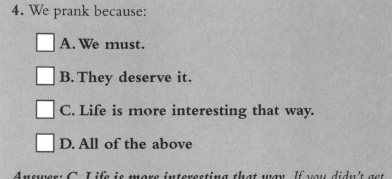

C. Disguise yourself as a park ranger and burst into another classroom. Explain that you are a visiting environmentalist who has arranged for all hall monitors to hand out free ducks. Slip into the nurse's office after the hall monitors are sufficiently mobbed.

Answer: A. The borwoolie ache. You avoid the hall monitors altogether, and practice your Confusey skills on the nurse.

6. Which of the following should you **never** do in the event of a full-scale invasion on your hideout by carnivorous cleaning ladies?

A. Lock all the doors and windows and set all your booby traps to "Super Sensitive." Find a comfortable place to hide. Don't move.

B. Stack all your dirty dishes in the dirtiest room in the lair. Wait until they all converge on the stack and cut a hole in the floor directly beneath them.

C. Activate the telescoping legs of your lair. Command it to leave the area immediately.

Answer: B. Stack the dishes. Cleaning ladies are too cunning to fall for this obvious bait.

7. When your mayor unlocks the door to his office in the morning, a herd of elk knocks him over as they stampede out. When you are rounded up for questioning, you say: ▶

☐ A. "I don't work with elk. It's not my medium."

☐ B. "Elk? Are you sure? Not something more practical like pigs or goats or something?"

☐ C. "Oh, I filled the mayor's office all right... with gerbils! And if there were no gerbils in that office this morning, then those elk are murderers!"

☐ D. "Elk? That's brilliant! I mean, isn't that the funniest thing you've ever heard? Whoever did that was a genius, don't you think?"

Answer: A. "Not my medium." If you've been rounded up by police, then they already know you're a practicing Mischievist. And though they tend to pursue us to the ends of the earth, the members of law enforcement appreciate miscreants who are true artists—sorry, artistes. *Sound like a snob, and you'll convince them.*

8. The sleeping-potion dart you're working on fails to put your brother to sleep after he is struck. Instead of dozing off, he becomes enraged and chases you with a long-handled broom. What's missing from your formula?

☐ A. An amphipathic lipid such as $CH_3(CH_2)_3$

☐ B. Biosynthesized tryptophan

☐ C. A tincture of carbonated dihydrogen monoxide, phosphoric acid, and grenadine

☐ D. Sweat socks

Answer: B. Tryptophan is an essential amino acid that induces sleep. Obviously.

9. What direction are Edgar's eyes pointing on page 38 of this book?

☐ **A. Toward safety**

☐ **B. Away from the squirrel**

☐ **C. Edgar is not on page 38.**

☐ **D. There is no page 38 in this book.**

Answer: E. None of the above. Just because we didn't give you option E, that doesn't mean you cannot select it. You are a Mischievist; regular rules do not apply to you.

SCORING:

9: Well done. Don your footie pajamas at once and report to E & E headquarters.

7–8: Pretty good. Disassemble and reassemble a Type 3 short-range catapult in less than three minutes and you're in the club.

4–6: Meh. We've seen better. Go back to page 1…by reading this book backward from the end of this sentence: Sit on a potato pan, Otis!

1–3: You're strictly Medgar & Melanie material, bub. Beat it before you get hurt around here.

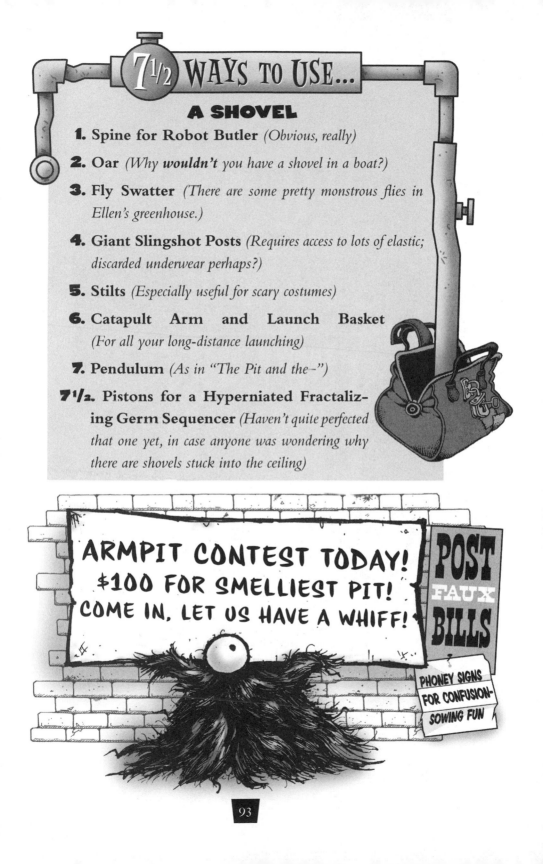

7½ WAYS TO USE...

A SHOVEL

1. Spine for Robot Butler *(Obvious, really)*

2. Oar *(Why **wouldn't** you have a shovel in a boat?)*

3. Fly Swatter *(There are some pretty monstrous flies in Ellen's greenhouse.)*

4. Giant Slingshot Posts *(Requires access to lots of elastic; discarded underwear perhaps?)*

5. Stilts *(Especially useful for scary costumes)*

6. Catapult Arm and Launch Basket *(For all your long-distance launching)*

7. Pendulum *(As in "The Pit and the—")*

7½. Pistons for a Hyperniated Fractaliz-ing Germ Sequencer *(Haven't quite perfected that one yet, in case anyone was wondering why there are shovels stuck into the ceiling)*

ARMPIT CONTEST TODAY!
$100 FOR SMELLIEST PIT!
COME IN, LET US HAVE A WHIFF!

POST FAUX BILLS

PHONEY SIGNS FOR CONFUSION-SOWING FUN

𝕿HERE. THE SCHEMATICS ARE REVEALED, your tests are completed, you've seen inside our heads. Now you know what we know. Okay, so maybe your guile or your cleverosity won't measure up to *ours*…but in terms of raw pranking power, we're on equal footing.

We've done our part . . . now it's your turn.

Look, the League of Mischievists isn't some club that meets after school from time to time where you show off the sweater you've knitted since the last meeting. If you want the respect (and fear) of your fellow pranksters, you have to keep busy. *Keep your skills sharp.* That means taking what you've learned from this book and putting it to good use.

So, you've spied a museum security guard too busy working on his unfinished novel to pay attention to you? Give *Operation: Tour de Farce* a try.

You're strolling down the street and find a psychic open for business? Stop in and try some cold reading on *her*.

You're slithering like a snake in the park and you notice a churro vendor with his back turned? Try a prank you've invented *yourself.*

Your definition of "good" may vary. —Edgar

Well, you know what we want you to *think* we know. —Ellen

You've lost me here, Ellen. —Edgar

Oh, at least *try* to keep up, Brother. —Ellen

But be ready. Membership in the League also carries with it the responsibility of service to us, your leaders. Some day—any day—you may find a crinkled note under your pillow or at the bottom of your cereal bowl, one that says something like, "Wrap your head in tinfoil and step outside your door at exactly 10 p.m.," or maybe, "Come to the mall at once; wear bug repellent and bring a bag of sugar cubes."

When that happens, don't ask questions, don't wonder why— just follow your instructions to the letter. Remember, the League is out there, ever planning, and when we need a cog or some boots to help us out, you'll hear from us. Be prepared to pull your weight. After all, you're a Mischievist now.

You're one of us.

Ooh, Edgar—does this mean "Operation: Blood, Sweets, & Tears" is almost ready for zero hour? —Ellen

Patience, grasshopper. —Edgar

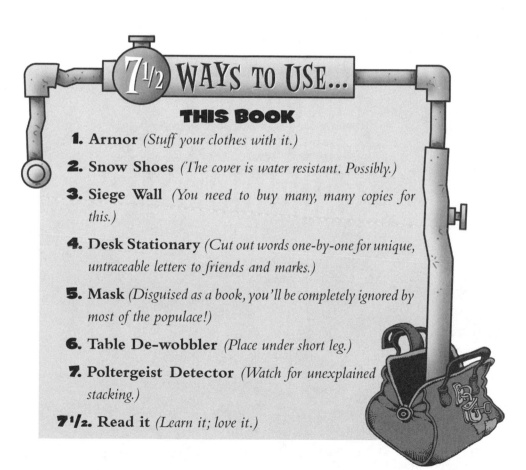

7½ WAYS TO USE...

THIS BOOK

1. Armor *(Stuff your clothes with it.)*

2. Snow Shoes *(The cover is water resistant. Possibly.)*

3. Siege Wall *(You need to buy many, many copies for this.)*

4. Desk Stationary *(Cut out words one-by-one for unique, untraceable letters to friends and marks.)*

5. Mask *(Disguised as a book, you'll be completely ignored by most of the populace!)*

6. Table De-wobbler *(Place under short leg.)*

7. Poltergeist Detector *(Watch for unexplained stacking.)*

7½. Read it *(Learn it; love it.)*

Ⓣ**HE LANGUAGE OF MISDEEDS** is a rich collection of tactical jargon and neat-sounding phrases. Learning to speak like a professional is a thrilling part of your education in the Mischief Arts.

Abigail: an innocent bystander utilized in a prank unbeknownst to her—or him; Abigails can be guys or gals.

abram men: pretend mad men. Useful in some of the more elaborate classic grifts, such as *The Rabid Organ Grinder* and *Operation: Nuts to You*

awake: aware of the scheme that's happening, especially against the will of the Mischievist. As in *"Better move on to another rube; this one's awake."*

bumpkin: see *clod*

bunko: fraud. Official police departments devoted to rooting out scams are known as Bunko Squads. Avoid these at all costs: they're awake to your dodge.

can opener: one who can open locks on safes; a safe-cracker

clod: see *hayseed*

comeuppance: what self-righteous people feel you deserve for being a prankster

Quoth me: "You are such a dummkopf, Edgar." —Ellen

Oh, come off it, Edgar. This puffed-up mumbo-jumbo just makes you feel important. Admit it. —Ellen

Quoth Edgar Allan Poe: "Words: The fancier they come, the awesomer they are." —Edgar

cracksman: a home-entry specialist (especially when ringing the doorbell and saying "May I come in?" isn't an option)

dished up: totally ruined. *"Your incorrect calculations really dished that one up, Edgar."*

doctors: alterations to an ordinary object to result in hilarious trouble for their owners. *"They put the doctors on him, and now his shoes won't stay on his feet."*

dry run: the act of practicing the operation before zero hour. If you're just going to soak a bunch of hula-hoopers with a fire hydrant, there is no need for a dry run. But if you've got eight different positions from which you need to launch smelly garbage within sixty seconds, you might want to give it a go.

duck soup: something that is extraordinarily easy

ABOUT GUARDING THE SECRET WORDS

Refer to the Mischievists' Code, Section 176-671 A2a★d: *"With regard to the Glossary definitions of prankster terminology: It is required that all Mischievists, upon gaining full member status in the League, hold these terms in secret. Comeuppance against the violation of the secrecy of these terms is to be determined by the nearest twin with pigtails. Proper usage of these closely guarded terms shall be defined as (a) able to shout the term/word/phrase while under duress with panache (i.e. flair, or 'coolness'); and (b) able to respond appropriately to shouted word under duress with appropriate jargon. 'Panache' shall be determined by its degree of similarity in vocalization pattern to the corresponding match of the aforementioned twin."*

gaffle: to scam or fool someone. As in: *"I got gaffled by a couple of pajama-wearing twins running the old Three-Nose Monte game. I'm such a rube."*

green, the: short for "green light"; the silent signal that everything is ready to go. Possible greens: the Thumbs-Up; the Wink; the Nose Honk; the Nose-Honk-Wink-and-Thumbs-Up; Fifteen Jumping Jacks

hayseed: see *rube*

ice: To be "put on ice" is to be distracted, held up, or kept away. *"The plan went south because the boots got put on ice by an old lady asking directions."*

inside: To come inside is to be let in on a plan. *"It's okay, we can talk. Pet's inside now."*

lever man: the guy who flips the switch

lullyprig: to borrow clothes off someone else's clothesline. Many a Mischievist has narrowly escaped a pursuer thanks to a quick lullyprig and a phony accent.

machinations: (MASH-uh-NAY-shunz) your plans; the sum total of all your brainy work on any scheme. A great-sounding word to use while performing a monologue for an imaginary audience in your lab, as in *"You were powerless against my machinations, Mr. Killgrave."*

nose: to figure out. *"If he noses out what we're up to, we'll need to go to Plan B."*

outs, on the: to be excluded from something, often something once included in. *"He ratted on us and now he's on the outs."*

Edgar really does this. He doesn't think I can hear him. —Ellen

packet: a false report, a bunch of lies. *"He wanted to know what we were up to all day, but I passed him a packet."*

pinched: caught. As in, don't get.

Reuben: a fun name to call your victim right in front of his face, and he'll never know it. *"Ellen, this is Reuben. He's the new rube—I mean, the new kid on the block."*

rube: see *sap*

rumble: to figure out the con. As in: *"They've rumbled the Phony Tour Guide bit. Cheese it!"*

sand: grit, the right stuff, a belly of steel. *"Miles'll never make it. Kid's got no sand."*

sap: see *yokel*

schadenfreude: happiness derived from the misery of others

snooter: ever-lingering doubt. *"Edgar, we should cheese it. I can't shake the snooter."*

the take: the booty; the prize; the great grab

whisker: a great lie. *"I'd better come up with a real whisker if I don't want to end up pulling up dandelions in detention."*

wild goose chase: see *yokel*

wolf in the stomach: to have a great appetite for mischief

yokel: see *bumpkin*

zucker: the kind of person who reads every word in a glossary

For Even More
Mischief and Mayhem,
Catch

Edgar & Ellen®
on
Nicktoons Network

And add to the adventure at
www.edgarandellen.com!

Edgar & Ellen books are also available from
Scholastic Audio

Read where the mischief begins...

BOOK 1

Edgar & Ellen:
Rare Beasts

BOOK 2

Edgar & Ellen:
Tourist Trap

BOOK 3

Edgar & Ellen:
Under Town

BOOK 4

Edgar & Ellen:
Pet's Revenge

BOOK 5

Edgar & Ellen:
High Wire

BOOK 6

Edgar & Ellen:
Nod's Limbs